"Findley writes, as ever, with compassion and patience. It is a measure of his humanity that he does not measure the worth of his characters. He does them the greater service of heedfulness."

Tim Wynne-Jones, *The Globe and Mail*

"A child dies, a plane crashes, an affair begins, a motorcycle roars through the rain, a boy's sexuality emerges—Findley writes of these things, the events of life and war, with sympathy and simplicity. More than anything, he wants to tell us that our stories matter. And he proves that they do."

Charles Gordon, *The Ottawa Citizen*

"The dislocations, fears and frustrations of a society at war are all here, wrapped in a glow, not quite nostalgic, that renders them at once vividly present and oddly far away. ... In *You Went Away*, not a shot is fired in anger. But the destructive hand of war has gripped its characters as surely as if they lived in occupied France."

John Bemrose, *Maclean's*

"... a fleeting tale that resonates in the mind long after the book's been put back on the shelf."

Skana Gee, *The Daily News* (Halifax)

"*You Went Away* is episodic, anecdotal; a series of vignettes rendered with a brevity and clarity that recall Imagist poetry and the sparse dramas of Harold Pinter."

John Moore, *The Vancouver Sun*

YOU WENT AWAY

A NOVELLA

TIMOTHY FINDLEY

HarperPerennial
HarperCollins*Publishers*Ltd

http://www.harpercollins.com/canada

First published in hardcover by HarperCollins Publishers Ltd: 1996
First HarperPerennial edition: 1997

Canadian Cataloguing in Publication Data

Findley, Timothy 1930–
     You went away : a novella

1st HarperPerennial ed.
ISBN 0-00-648099-3

I. Title.

PS8511.I38Y68 1997   C813'.54   C97-930341-9
PR9199.3.F52Y68 1997

97 98 99 ❖ HC 10 9 8 7 6 5 4 3 2 1

Printed and bound in the United States

For
Al and Nora Joyce
and in memory
of
Agnes Mortson
and
Edna Mott

This is not their story —
but it was their war ...

You went away,
And my heart went with you ...

"You'll Never Know"
Mack Gordon and Harry Warren

ACKNOWLEDGEMENTS

Fiction is rooted in fact. For many of the facts about the times and locations of this story, I am indebted to the thorough and inspired research of Beverley Roberts. For invaluable information about the R.C.A.F., I am grateful to Terence Macartney-Filgate, Ted Barris and Lyle Greenlaw and to Keith Lawson, Base Borden Military Museum and Archives. As always, I want to acknowledge the efforts of the staff of the Metropolitan Toronto Reference Library who, despite funding cutbacks, continue to maintain the library's invaluable resources and to facilitate public access. And finally, I thank those who each make a unique contribution to the creation of my books: Iris Tupholme, for her perception of what the second-last draft needs — and the tact with which she tells me; Mary Adachi, for her meticulous and creative copy-editing — and the superb meal that accompanies it; William Whitehead, for his patience, his enthusiasm — and for denying me the use of our word-processor, with which — given how easy it renders revision — I would probably never get past page one.

In the flea market, a shoe box filled with photographs. This is all we have. Whose lives might be recovered, if only the box had been labelled?

This book is such a box, retrieved from the past. Faces pulled in handfuls back into the light. Revealed by twos and threes and dozens — this and this and these. The lives no longer whole, but torn; fragmented. Here, for instance:

A man and a woman walking in the rain. We cannot and may never see their faces. They walk beneath an umbrella, stepping smartly away from us. The rain that falls around them is barely visible — recognized more by the sheen on the umbrella than by the actual shape of its descent. A warm rain — or cold. A summer rain — a winter fall of snow. All these are possibilities, but there is nothing here of certainty — only away. That is what we see. They walk — they direct their whole attention to departure.

And who would take such a picture? To whom would this leavetaking mean so much that a record must be made of it? They were mine. Now they are going — gone.

Or perhaps: I was theirs and they left me, stranded. Abandoned. *Or perhaps: we'll be standing at the corner, waiting for you to catch us up. This is what you hope the image says — but something tells you no. The man and the woman will not return. They are leaving together, but not for the same destination. Even as she touches his arm, something in the woman's gesture says:* at the corner, we will part.

Maybe. Maybe not.

The box itself has been destroyed beyond recovery. Time and the elements have done their work. Nothing remains to tell you who these people are.

1

Or were. We know that some of them are dead — *dying gently or killed. We know this because they disappear all at once and do not return to stand beside the people with whom they were formerly seen. Also, there are pictures of a grave. On the grave, the name is indecipherable, blurred by flowers set down before the stone in baskets, urns and wreaths. This person was greatly loved. And yet, no mourners are visible here, only what they have brought as tribute* — *ferns and roses, lilies, chrysanthemums.*

Some of the photographs were taken so entirely in another time it is doubtful anyone remains alive who could give them meaning. Turn-of-the-century motorcars, women carrying furs and wearing large unwieldy hats, men in high white collars, boys in shorts and long black stockings — *all the jackets cut with an air of jauntiness* — *some with belted backs.*

Then, there are soldiers, laughing, making faces at the camera, while they bond together, clasping one another shoulder to shoulder in groups of four and six and eight. This can only be 1914–18. More departures. More forevers.

Sports day, perhaps as early as 1917 — *perhaps as late as 1925. Runners in white, muddied and smiling, winners all* — *or so it seems. These are boys, not quite young men. The girls are dressed in heavy sweaters* — *cardigans* — *and they wear long scarves. Field hockey, 1912 perhaps* — *you cannot tell.* Maisie or Rose or Anne Marie *is standing, arms akimbo* — *captain of the team. Later you will recognize her* — *posing as a flapper, wearing fringe and impossible shoes.*

A man and a woman marry. There are bridesmaids standing in a row and sombre-looking fathers, nervous mothers and furious siblings got up in Eton suits and velvet dresses — *desperately uncomfortable, jealous of the adult world with its privileges of choosing one's own clothes and slouching, if one so desires. Everyone stands up ramrod straight.* Smile, *they are no doubt told, but this is ritual* — *no one smiles.*

All of these scenes take place in cities — *more than likely Toronto or Montreal. You know this by the formal shapes of the houses and their placement beyond the sidewalks. Lawns and flowerbeds abound — high-cut hedges — privacy guaranteed. Tramways speak of large populations — people crowded onto the cars, someone running — always someone running to get on board. Streets with crowds of people bent on being somewhere else:* I'm late. I must hurry. I will miss the sale — the spectacle — my lover.

Then, all at once, a single image, seemingly out of place. A young man wearing running shorts and shirtless. All of Saskatchewan — possibly all of Manitoba — is spread out behind him. All of the prairie, all of the prairie sky and nothing, no one else. His posture tells you he is shy of cameras. Or perhaps of the photographer.

Children, also — here in the 1930s — boys in "breeks," breeches tied at the knee with laces, sweaters, stockings, everything itchy — woolen and heavy; girls in cotton dresses, unadorned and staring. The women now wear smaller hats, white gloves and simple suits — the men are dressed in grey and blue. The faces here are serious, furrowed, squinting. In the background, once or twice, we see a dark-hued Franklin with a rumble seat and running-boards. It is parked on a tree-lined street, and its canvas top is down.

Then the war returns — the ever-present war that began with the Boers in 1899 and ran its course until 1945 — empires ending, others ascending. Uniforms again — modified — modern. Still the same old colours — white and blue and khaki — but not the same old lines. Somehow, they are less professional — looser, baggier. Even the generals have less austerity. Leaders of the Free World, flaunting cigarettes, ride in wheelchairs or, wearing "siren suits," smoke cigars.

Something frantic happens. Not again. We can't. *But they do. Here is the prairie sprinter, dressed in leather, standing by a motorcycle. Here are a father and son. You have seen them before. They stand, in skates, on a back-yard rink, their hockey sticks held like pilgrims' staves while a host of other boys surround them. Here are a mother and daughter, circa 1938. They are seated side by side on a bench in a park somewhere. The mother wears a small, neat hat and a formal suit of some dark colour. The daughter, dressed as a boy, is carrying a teddy bear. The corners of its mouth are stitched to suggest a smile* — *and yet, the bear is as solemn as the girl.* We are having our picture taken; please behave. *All three face the camera as if alone on the bench. And then you see the daughter's hand, behind the bear* — *holding tight to her mother's sleeve.*

A woman with square-cut hair is standing before an easel. She wears a painter's smock and running shoes. Only her body is present. Her mind, with its images, is far away — *elsewhere. Clearly, she has only consented to be photographed because she trusts the photographer.* Please don't make too much of this — it's only me.

Lastly, circa 1939 or '40, a man and a woman dressed in party clothes. She might be a movie star, her presence is so keen. She wears the kind of evening gown that then was called provocative: *strapless, deeply cut and revealing. He is tall and wears white tie and tails. If Gary Cooper was unavailable, this man might have been his stand-in. She looks at him* — *almost his equal in height* — *with humour and with awe.* How did we get so lucky? *Shadowed and standing behind them, we can see the mother without her daughter, the father without his son.* One last carefree time, and then to war.

All of this tells — *begins to tell* — *a story. Some few connections can be made. Sequence is difficult. This before this* — *or after? And who is that? Someone's sister* — *someone's aunt, perhaps.*

Time might have claimed them all. But these were saved, bought and sold in a Sunday market. Fragments only — *reaching backward, trying to connect* — *to become complete again.*

This and this and these — *no other. There is nothing more than what is here. The remnants* — *not the remains. The pieces* — *not the whole.*

Not a puzzle, but a patchwork of unstitched lives.

Two walk away. It rains. Was their story over — or just beginning? A man and a woman, trailing their lives behind them — neither of them turning for one last look, neither of them waving goodbye. Stepping forward — where are we going? And what comes after? Have we forgotten something? Will we be remembered?

Have we been seen?

Yes.

3rd September, 1939

On Sundays, they met for tea at Ellen's. Her home was on Foxbar Road in the city of Toronto.

Matthew, who would be nine in October, was intrigued by the view from the high board fence in Ellen's backyard. There was a cemetery there and, sitting in his blue Sunday suit, he could watch the families of the dead bringing flowers to the graves. On occasion, there would be other children and Matthew would wave at them. Most waved back, but some did not. Those who did not looked at him as if he must be crazy.

Waving at strangers was one of Matthew's pastimes. It allowed him to be seen. *Hello.* But he never said it. Other pastimes were feeding the horses on the way to school and, in the summer, walking along the fences through his neighbours' backyards. He never tired of other people's private lives. He also read books and listened to the radio. This way, he could be anyone he chose to be: *Rob the Ranger, Mowgli* or *Jim Hawkins.*

Sundays were otherwise uneventful. Sometimes they went to church, but most times not. Matthew's father, Graeme Forbes, never went. He had given up believing when his brother died. But on occasion, Matthew and his sister, Bonnie, would accompany their mother to St. Paul's Anglican Church on Bloor Street. *Just to keep in touch*, their mother would say with a smile. Her name was Michael, but people called her *Mi*. Mi as in *my blue heaven*.

Bonnie was five. Matthew adored her. She was the heroine of all his stories — honey-haired, blue-eyed and more than willing to be endangered. She would go with you anywhere and play whatever role you assigned her. *You've fainted and I have to save you from a burning house filled with explosives. You're a captive — tied to a tree — and I have to rescue you before the pirates come back.* Now, he was teaching her how to be a spy. This meant Bonnie had to sneak all the way from her bedroom after dark to the kitchen — without being seen or heard. The object was to capture a chocolate brownie or a peanut butter cookie and bring it back to him as proof of her success.

Today, the cemetery had only one family in it. No children, just adults. They brought white flowers and put them on a grave and crossed themselves and stood there looking awkward, saying nothing. Matthew did not wave.

Mi came to the back door and said: "we're ready, hon."

This meant food.

Matthew jumped down and hurried over the grass. He could smell the cheese-and-bacon toasts that were one of Ellen's specialties. They were always served in a silver dish with a cover.

In the living-room, everyone was silent. Matthew wondered if Ellen had told them all not to speak. She could be like that — domineering. Deadly.

Ellen Forbes was Matthew's grandmother. She lived with his father's sister, Auntie Isabel. Also present were distant cousins, Lewis and Loretta Benson. Loretta always wore a hat and dresses with flowing sleeves and billowing skirts. Lewis was losing his hair and wore bow-ties.

Bonnie was sitting on the floor underneath the tea table. Her bear was with her. It had no name. Just *Bear*. Bonnie sat cross-legged in her white muslin dress, looking worried. *When is Matthew going to come and rescue me?*

All along the mantel, there were photographs and objects that had to do with Ellen's dead husband, Tom, and her dead son, Ian.

Ian had been Isabel's twin. He was killed in the Great War — shot down out of the sky in a Camel aeroplane. In one of the photographs, he stood beside its propeller and leaned against its wing, wearing a long white scarf and smiling Isabel's crooked smile.

The mantelpiece was Ellen's sacred shrine. Isabel said: *you don't exist unless she puts you there. Comes in here and practically genuflects — practically gets on her knees in front of those photographs. All but crosses herself.* The dead — excluding the living.

Tea was poured. Bonnie was handed a glass of milk. Matthew had ginger ale. Sandwiches were served, which Matthew carried about on their plates, offering them to the adults, who were seated. There was also the silver dish of cheese-and-bacon toasts.

Graeme never sat down in his mother's house. When Matthew had arrived in the living-room, his father had not been there. He had gone upstairs to use the washroom. Now, he returned and said: "more bad news."

From the bathroom?

Everyone looked so glum.

"What more can there possibly be?" This was Ellen.

"Has anyone told Mattie what's going on? He's looking a little baffled." This was Lewis.

"We decided not to tell him, till we knew more." This was Mi.

"*What?*" Matthew.

"England has declared war on Germany." Isabel.

Oh.

Matthew said: "I thought it was over."

Isabel smiled. "No, dear. That was the other war."

Mi said: "Mattie — come here."

She was seated on the sofa beside Loretta. She wore a pale blue summer dress that matched her eyes. Her face was square and solemn. *What's going to happen? What?* Matthew stood in front of her and she straightened his tie. "You aren't to be afraid," she said.

"Are they coming here? The Germans?"

"No, hon. And they won't. We're not at war yet. Only England."

"England and France," said Graeme. "And we're sure to follow."

Loretta said: "I do hope America won't. The last war played blue havoc with my whole family — and all those dear dead boys I used to dance with." She reached out for Lewis, but he evaded her.

Matthew looked at his father. Why did he never sit down? There was a glass of something in his hand, but that was not unusual — though he normally didn't drink in front of his mother. He was her youngest child and the only son who had survived. When the Great War ended, he was just fifteen. Ellen did not seem to approve of his survival. His picture was not on the mantel with the heroes. Women considered him extremely handsome, with his satyr's eyes and honey, flyaway hair. Matthew worshipped him from a necessary distance. Graeme did not have a great deal to say to either of his children. Now, in Ellen's living-room, standing in sunlight, he said: "the sooner we jump, the sooner it will be over."

Ellen was silent. She looked at the mantelpiece and lighted a cigarette. Matthew watched her sitting in her traditional corner under the portrait of his grandfather. Her blue-tinted hair and slitted eyes were almost hidden behind the veil of smoke from her cigarette. Her "tea" was sherry, but Matthew didn't know this. She drank it from a cup.

Isabel said: "you said there was more bad news."

Graeme said: "yes. I wanted to hear what was happening, so I turned on the radio in Mother's room while I was up there ..."

"What?" said Lewis. "For heaven's sake, what?"

"They've sunk a ship," said Graeme. "A passenger ship. *The Athenia*."

"Who? Who sank it?"

"The Germans. In the Irish Sea."

"But the war is only one day old. Not even that," said Loretta.

"A passenger ship?" said Mi.

"Yes. And coming here. She was going to land in Montreal."

"Oh, God." Mi had grown up in Montreal. Outremont.

"That means Canadians would have been on board."

"Yes. A good many."

Matthew sagged, leaning back against Mi, standing between her knees. She put her arms around him and he thought: *this is not a story*.

Suddenly, Ellen spoke.

"How many?" she said.

"They don't know yet," said Graeme. "It happened in the dark. They're still trying to find survivors."

Survivors.

Swimming in the dark.

Matthew looked at Uncle Ian in his uniform on the mantel.

Everyone dies in a war. There are no survivors.

"What will happen?" said Isabel.

"We must pray for them," said Loretta.

"Not in this house, you won't," said Ellen.

Everyone stared at her.

"If there is a God — He's mad. I renounce Him. All this again. WASN'T ONCE ENOUGH! WASN'T *ONCE* ENOUGH!"

Mi's arms tightened around Matthew. Neither of them had ever heard Ellen raise her voice in such a manner. She seemed possessed.

Under the table, Bonnie began to cry.

"I don't want to drown," she said. "I don't want to drown."

Mi let Matthew go, stood up and crossed the room.

Stooping in front of the table, she put out her hand, took Bonnie's glass of milk and set it on the tray. Then she said: "come out, hon. Come out from under."

Bonnie crawled forward, dragging Bear, and stood up.

"I think we should go home," Mi said.

Graeme nodded.

No one else moved.

Bonnie was rocking Bear in her arms.

War again. Another war, already claiming its dead in the sea. Matthew went and put his finger on Uncle Ian's face in the photograph. *That's what happens. Everybody dies.* He walked away and stood beside the window. *How can the sun be shining?*

Nobody spoke.

Ellen emptied her cup and, rising, started for the dining-room where the sherry bottle hid in its cupboard, waiting for her. On her way, she paused by the mantel and turned all the photographs face down. Eight of them.

"Enough is enough," she said. "Enough is enough."

9th September, 1939

The following Saturday, Canada entered the war. To celebrate, Graeme drove them out to Malton Airport on the western limits of the city. There, he chose what turned out to be the last free space at the side of the road, and parked.

"Lucky us," he said. He was beaming. They had come — like dozens of others — to see the aeroplanes, a summer Saturday tradition.

On the way, they had stopped to buy gasoline, cigarettes and Coca-Cola. These provided the tastes and smells Matthew always associated with summer drives and his parents' love affair. Not that he called it a *love affair*, but only that it was — or seemed to be — the stuff of which he read in *Lamb's Tales from Shakespeare* and saw in the movies. Greeting always with a kiss. His mother taking his father's arm as they walked or leaning against his shoulder while he drove. Ways, too, in which they glanced at one another — especially Mi at Graeme — with sudden, knowing smiles. Also, their laughter. Their ease in one another's presence. Though it was fading — their closeness — the heady fumes of gasoline had been a part of it — and the taste of Coca-Cola, the smell of cigarette smoke and the sight of his parents' wind-blown hair, the strands intermingled as they drove. Also, the cool, padded leatherette of the Franklin's rumble seat and the heat-dried smell of its lowered canvas top.

Bonnie and Bear had stood up on the way and were told to sit down. *Never stand on the seat of a moving car.* Yes, sir.

At Malton, safely parked, they all stood up on the seats and waved at incognito pilots flying red and yellow aeroplanes: one with what

12

seemed a painted mannequin in the cockpit — goggled, helmeted, scarved and expressionless; another with its long-haired, wind-blown lady and yet one more with its sun-glassed, smiling twins. Who were all these flying strangers? That was part of the romance.

The day was September-perfect — a high, wide cloudless sky and all the wind socks drooping; warm, but not oppressively hot; languid, but redolent of possibilities. Anything might happen. After all, a war had been declared — an enemy might appear and a battle ensue. Certainly, the antics in the air had taken on a playful *war-iness*, if such a word exists. Chasings and paired formations with overtones of remembered *dog-fights* over France — remembered or reconstructed from the stuff of all those air-ace legends, now the folklore of a generation. *Bishop, Collishaw, Martin ... Richthofen*, rising up in pursuit of one another — turning, turning — always turning — dancing in the sky.

"It was a war between gentlemen," Graeme told them. "Every time an enemy fell, he was given a salute."

Mi looked away.

Graeme said: "if a German pilot was killed and crashed behind our lines, he received a military funeral. All the honours, including a firing party."

"What's a firing party?" Matthew asked

"When soldiers die, a squad of riflemen fire into the sky above the grave. It's the ultimate tribute. That — and 'The Last Post,' which a bugler plays."

"If Uncle Ian had crashed behind the German lines, would they have done that for him?"

"Of course. Yes."

Mi turned and looked at Bonnie.

"Comfy?"

"Unh-hunh."

"And Bear?"

"Unh-hunh."

"Matthew?"

"Yes, ma'am."

Mi faced the sky.

"What a lovely, heavenly day," she said.

Graeme said: "we will always remember this. The day we entered the war and came out here to watch the aeroplanes."

Far away an engine faltered. Everyone fell silent.

In all the cars parked out along the road, drivers and passengers stood up and stared — almost a hundred people, shading their eyes from the sun.

"Turn," Graeme whispered. "*Turn! Turn over!*"

They waited.

Nothing.

Turn.

And then it did. With a bang and a stutter, the engine flared back to life. Everyone cheered. It was a perfect afternoon.

After the aeroplanes, Graeme took them out to dinner at Murray's on Yonge Street, south of Bloor. Matthew could see the marquee of the Uptown Theatre. *Dark Victory* — with Bette Davis.

Graeme was in the best of moods. "We're in," he said, sitting down in the restaurant, "and we're going to win."

Earlier in the summer they had been to Shanty Bay up north of the city, where a cottage was rented most years for July and August. There was a dock in the bay at the end of their road and a diving board with three heights. Off the top, the descent into the water was twenty feet and this was Graeme's purview. The sun was worshipped, everyone swam — except Bonnie — and Mi made up a suntan lotion of olive oil and vinegar. Consequently, sitting together in Murray's that Sunday night, Graeme and Mi and their children, wearing white, were the picture of bronzed and athletic health. Several people stared at them. *Who can they be?*

Matthew ordered the Club House Sandwich — his all-time favourite restaurant food — and Bonnie had a children's plate of Chicken à la King. Mi and Graeme had Salisbury Steak, with a rich, dark gravy and French fried potatoes. Later, they would walk up Yonge Street and all day tomorrow it would be Sunday.

Graeme said: "look at these people. Everyone smiling. Every one of them knows it will be over before you can count to ten."

"*Ten*," said Mi — and laughed. "Well, Gray — is it over yet?"

Graeme did not smile. He glanced away and fingered his glass. Tomato juice. Later — perhaps — something else at home.

"You kids okay?" he said.

"Why can't Bear come to Murray's?" Bonnie asked. Even though small for her age, she no longer had to sit in a high chair. This was a triumph. *I'm not a Munchkin any more!*

"Bears aren't allowed in restaurants," said Mi.

"Why?"

"They eat people."

Matthew laughed.

"Sometimes," Mi added.

Graeme, who had been looking over their fellow diners, said: "in two weeks time, this room will be full of uniforms."

Yes.

"In two weeks time, Yonge Street will look like a river of khaki and blue. I remember that from before — the other time — the last war. A river of uniforms." He looked at Mi. "Was Montreal the same?"

"Yes. You couldn't move. We were a port, of course. The coming and going was constant."

Graeme pushed his empty plate away — sat back and lighted a cigarette. "What a moment," he said. "What a moment. What a day."

He was jubilant. The feeling in his body was the same as it had been at school when he walked out onto the field and saw the opposing team assembled, knowing he was king of the line, feared and revered and worshipped. Now, he sat with his family in the midst of another vibrant throng, watching his wife and children caught and embraced in the sweep of his glance. He loved them — all at once, entirely — with a pride that would slowly vanish and a need for their presence in his life that would slowly be denied. But that came later. Not that he was claiming ownership or saying *mine* with his possessive glance, but something more profound. He was saying: *us*. And he was happy. *Us*, for the very last time.

Their house, which they rented, was on Crescent Road. It cost them twenty-four dollars a month. Mi counted every penny. It was her ambition to buy the house one day and live there forever. After her parents' divorce, it had fed her need for stability, with its sunny rooms and its mock orange hedge and its roses along the walk. She even loved its leaky roof and the bats in its attic. *Atmosphere,* she called it. *A place must have atmosphere if you're going to be happy there.*

The trouble was, Graeme wouldn't buy the house. Not that he hated it, just that he didn't want to own anything. After their losses in the Great Depression, he had said: *I'm through with owning things. You only lose them in the long run.* This, at any rate, was his stand. But Matthew had a notion it was a lie. For one thing, his father never counted pennies, the way his mother did. He wasn't saving up for anything. He took his pennies with him downtown and often he didn't come home. Or, at least, he didn't come home when Matthew was awake.

Now, it was Matthew's ninth birthday, and Graeme had promised him a bicycle, even taking him the week before to Canadian Tire at the corner of Yonge and Davenport to look the selection over. Matthew had chosen a blue one with rubber grips on the handlebars. It was a C.C.M. That day, coming home, they had gone down into the park behind the house on Crescent Road and tossed a football — something they once did all the time. Now, for the most part, the football sat on Graeme's bureau or he would carry it with him into the living-room and finger it like a dog in his lap while he read the paper.

Matthew did not like birthday parties. They embarrassed him. But Mi made a cake and ordered ice cream from Hunt's and set out her gift and the gift she had bought for Bonnie to give him on the table and they waited.

Graeme's usual time of arrival from downtown was between five-thirty and six. That night, he still wasn't home at seven.

Matthew hung around the front hall, not knowing where he should be when his father came home with the bike. He could be up in his bedroom doing his homework: DRAW A MAP OF CANADA AND ALL THE PROVINCES' NAMES IN CAPITAL LETTERS. That way, he would have to be called down and could act "surprised" when he saw what Graeme had brought. Or he could put his windbreaker on and sit in the backyard and count the stars.

Where's Mattie, Mi?

He's sitting out there with the stars again. Night in, night out, counting, counting …

At seven-thirty Bonnie said: "ice cream. Now."

"Good idea," said Mi.

Matthew was sitting on the stairs. He had given up waiting.

"Hon?"

Matthew sighed.

Mi said: "I think we'd better go ahead without him, don't you? You have that map to draw and it's time for Bonnie to go to bed."

"Okay."

He wouldn't cry. At nine, you didn't. The last time he'd cried had been when Teddy Carter had thrown that puck and hit him in the face. Almost a year ago. His nose had bled and they couldn't stop it. In the end, Mi took him to Doctor Coombs, where his nose had been cauterized. Ice cream every night for a week.

In the dining-room, they were silent. Almost. Bonnie beat a tattoo on her plate and made a more or less constant humming noise while she ate.

Matthew had closed his eyes before blowing out his candles and conjured up the letters *C.C.M.*

No one spoke.

Matthew undid his packages — a box of crayons from Bonnie, *so you won't keep using up hers.* And from Mi, a short-sleeved sweater like the one George Fawcett wore — except that Matthew's sweater was blue.

Blue is Mother's colour, not mine. Except in bikes, he thought — and then, at last: "WHERE IS HE?"

Mi lied.

"There must be some kind of meeting," she said.

"Why can't he phone and say so?"

"It's all right, darling. Please." She glanced at Bonnie.

Don't upset your sister.

Matthew turned away.

"Thanks for the sweater," he said. And: "thanks for the crayons." Then he went up to his room and closed the door.

At nine, some car doors slammed and Graeme came home. He was not alone.

Matthew heard voices and went to stand at the top of the stairs. He was wearing his pyjamas and could feel the cold air rising from below as the men — there were five of them besides his father — took off their overcoats and shook them out.

"It's snowing," someone said. "First time in over ten years it's snowed in October."

Greetings were spoken, and introductions — all too loud and all with too much laughter.

Matthew waited. He even held his breath, so he wouldn't miss what came next. Any minute his father would say: *where's Mattie, Mi?* And his mother would come to the bottom of the stairs and call up: *Matthew* — very dignified and proper for a nine-year-old. *Matthew.* No one ever called him that — *but one day ...*

He sat down on the top step. *Come on, Dad. Call me.*

Nothing.

The men and their voices moved into the dining-room. Matthew could hear them getting out bottles and glasses.

What? What is it? Who? Who are they?

Laughter. And back-slapping.

Where was his mother?

Matthew stood up. He started down the stairs. He was an expert at this — at silence — barefooted, every creak and every pitfall memorized. Like an Indian — not a sound. The way he taught Bonnie.

He reached the landing and stopped just long enough to make sure the string on his pyjama pants was tied and the opening closed. He'd had that happen once when he was creeping — passing like a shadow through the hall, when he'd felt a sudden draught and realized his pyjama fly was open and Mrs Carroway, sitting on the living-room sofa, had seen his thing and giggled.

Now he could see the men with his father in the dining-room. He didn't know who they were — not one of them.

Dad?

He scouted the vestibule, thinking perhaps his father had left the bike there. But no.

He went out into the kitchen.

Mi was sitting at the table, smoking a cigarette and drinking a cup of tea.

"What's going on? Who are they?"

Mi spoke more to the cup than to Matthew. "Friends of your father's." She was obviously angry, but he did not know why. "Your father has something to tell you," she said.

"About my bike?"

Mi said nothing. She stubbed her cigarette and stood up.

"Come with me," she said.

She took his hand and led him into the pantry. Just before she pushed on past the swinging door, she stopped and looked at him and cupped his face in her hand.

"Hon — this will not be fun, and I'm sorry. But there's nothing we can do about it."

He stared at her.

"Okay?"

Matthew could barely whisper. "Okay."

Mi set her shoulder against the door and they went through.

All the men — who were in their shirt sleeves now, including his father — turned and saw them.

"This is Matthew, our son," said Mi. And then: "today is his birthday."

Everyone smiled and nodded and said things Matthew could not decipher. There was only one voice that mattered — and it was silent.

Matthew said: "Mum says you've something to tell me."

Graeme, looking strangely amused, put down his glass on the table, spilling its contents over the polish.

Matthew waited. Mi was behind him, one hand resting on his shoulder.

"Tell him," she said, her voice unfriendly.

Graeme winked at his friends before he spoke — and then stepped forward, putting out his hand.

Matthew looked at it, mute.

"Take it," his father said.

"Why?"

"Because you have to congratulate me."

Matthew very solemnly took his father's hand, shook it and set it free.

Now his father touched his own chest with his fingers and said: "I've joined the Air Force, Mattie. Me, and all these fellows here — we're going to win the war!"

Matthew stepped back.

His father went on smiling. Then he said: "Mi, honey — maybe you'd better take him up to his bed. We've got some more drinking to do down here."

Mi said nothing. She escorted Matthew past the others and into the hall and up the stairs.

At his door, she kissed the top of his head and said: "I'll buy the bicycle tomorrow."

"No," said Matthew. "*Don't*. It has to come from him."

Mi nodded and went downstairs.

For the next two hours all the strangers and his father sang old songs and shouted. Mi went back to the kitchen. The last thing Matthew heard that night was a song he would never forget. Next day he went down into the hall and picked it out, one-fingered, on the piano.

> *Oh, you'll take the high road*
> *And I'll take the low road,*
> *And I'll be in Scotland before you ...*

His father was playing. The singing was oddly hushed and sweet.

> *But me and my true love will never meet again,*
> *On the bonnie, bonnie banks of Loch Lomond.*

Beyond the windows, the snow gave way to rain.

Matthew slept. He dreamt of Bonnie running through a heather field. He also dreamt the sky.

Here is where the pictures lag behind events. In Europe, Norway, Denmark, France, the Netherlands and Belgium fell to Hitler's blitzkrieg. Matthew receives his bicycle, standing with it solo on the lawn. Bonnie falls and cuts her forehead. She and Bear are seated in winter light, sporting twin bandages. Michael and Graeme are seen in the springtime, side by side and arm in arm, unsmiling beside a lilac tree. She is in grey, he wears the uniform of a Flying Officer in the R.C.A.F. In the world at large, things go from bad to worse, but none of this is seen — except in the expressions on the faces. Something in the way they stare the camera down tells you they have lost their connection to one another. There is not a single photograph that shows them all together.

23rd September, 1940

A year passed, their lives in a state of constant flux that sometimes verged on chaos. Everyone was at the mercy of orders — *do this, don't do that. Go here, don't go there. Hurry up and wait.*

Graeme went away and came back and went away again. Briefly, he was posted to Toronto, which meant that he could live at home. But that was only for a month and they saw very little of him. He was in training for something he wouldn't talk about.

To Matthew, he seemed an entirely different man — which perhaps he was. His uniform made him look like everyone else. Gone the pale grey suits and green-flecked ties that matched his eyes. Gone the dark fedora with its feather and its tilt. Gone the hanky sprouting from his breast. Gone the overcoat in which he once took over the streets with his striding presence. And gone the boylike face with its mischievous smile. He had darkened now, and was hidden out of reach behind an expression Matthew could not read. *I am not your father any more,* it seemed to say. But this was inexplicable and unacceptable. Even in his presence, Matthew wanted to say to him: *come back.* But he was gone.

Graeme was constantly preoccupied — not with his Air Force duties, which seemed to bore him, but with something else, unnamed. Mi would sit watching him in the lamplight and he would say to her: *don't stare at me* — angry for some reason. Now, he was away again. In Halifax. Coastal Command.

On the 23rd of September, 1940, they were told that another passenger ship had been torpedoed on its way to Canada. Matthew heard about it on the radio. More than two hundred people were drowned — many of them children. Mi forbade him to speak of it to Bonnie. *She is so afraid of water. It's bad enough just trying to give her a bath.*

The next day, a Tuesday, Miss Bransby asked the whole class to stand and say a silent prayer for all the dead children, of whom there were eighty-seven. Matthew had counted them. Some of their pictures had been in the papers, but Bonnie was not allowed to see them. The ship was called *The City of Benares.* Seven of the children had been destined for Toronto. Matthew might have met them on the street — played with them in the schoolyard — asked them home for dinner. Now, not. Ever.

The night before Miss Bransby's prayer, Matthew had a dream — the first of a kind that would plague his sleep for weeks and months to come. In it, he was in a long, grey-lit corridor, against whose tilt he moved in slow motion while behind him water gathered without a sound. When he woke in the dark, his covers rose up over him like a wave and he threw them to the floor. From then on, he slept without them and wore two pairs of pyjamas and his hockey socks, instead.

30th October, 1940

Matthew had decided that the age of ten signalled the end of child-hood. For his birthday, he had asked Mi to give him a pair of long trousers.

When she told him this was not possible, he was astonished.

"Why?" he asked.

The truth was Mi could not afford them, but she didn't want to tell him that. Instead, she said that if he was willing to give up his allowance she might consider it. His allowance was twenty-five cents a week.

"Why would I have to give it up?"

"Well, you don't go around paying an allowance to people in long trousers," she said. "Any more than you'd buy them a comic book or treat them to a sundae. Any more than you'd take them to the Honey Dew, or give them a chocolate bar. Not any more than you'd ..."

"*Mum.*"

Mi had been prepared for the list to go on as long as it took him to understand. "People who wear long trousers pay their own way," she concluded. "So, if you're willing to pay your own way, what colour would you like? Grey flannels? Navy blue? Khaki? Which?"

"Never mind."

Matthew slumped in his chair, forced back into childhood by his measly allowance. He was furious.

Mi looked at him and smiled. They were seated in the kitchen.

"Would you settle for a new pair of breeks?" She had been going to buy them anyway.

"Sure." His voice was level and distant. Other people had long trousers. Greg Lawson. Steven Porter. It wasn't fair.

"How would you like a Club House Sandwich at Murray's?"

Matthew brightened.

"My treat," Mi said. "Happy birthday, my darling."

6th December, 1940

One Friday, Matthew came home from school and Mi was in the living-room talking to a stranger. She turned and said: "go to the kitchen, hon. I'll be out in a minute."

An elegant overcoat and scarf were draped beneath a brown fedora on the newel post at the foot of the stairs. From the kitchen Matthew heard the visitor come into the hall, collect his things and depart. The front door gave a sigh and, closing, the weight of it sent a shiver through the house.

When Mi did not immediately appear as she had promised, Matthew went back to look for her. He hadn't even taken off his windbreaker and still carried his toque. He stood in the front hall and called.

"Mum?"

"Just a minute."

She was in the dining-room. He could hear her closing the doors of the china cabinet and, when he went in, she was crouching in front of the buffet, pushing in its drawers — which always stuck.

"Damn," she said. "*Damn.*"

"What's wrong?"

"Nothing. Just the usual. They won't shut."

"You want me to do it?"

"No." She threw the word like a stone. Then she gave the bottom drawer a bang with her fist and shot it into place.

Matthew watched her. Instead of rising, she went on crouching there, her face turned away from him.

"You're home early," she said. "I wish you'd wait for me in the kitchen. Maybe you could put the kettle on. I won't be long."

"Sure."

Bewildered, he retreated.

Still in his windbreaker, still with his toque in his hand, Matthew grabbed the kettle from the stove and went to fill it. The sink stood sideways in an alcove, overshadowed by shelves of dishes.

To his right, he could see through the window into the back-yard. No rink this year. The war — and his absent father.

Graeme was still in Halifax. Now, it was getting on to Christmas. Maybe he would come home then — put up the boards and flood the yard with the hose, the way he normally did. The rink would be Matthew's Christmas present.

By now, the kettle had overflowed and Matthew lugged it across the room — spilling water all the way to the stove. Then he sat down at the kitchen table and stared at the doorway to the dining-room.

Mother? Mum?

He put his toque back on. It was wet and itchy against his fore-head. He counted to fifty. Where was Bonnie? He stood up and turned on the overhead light.

Come on, Mum — for Pete's sake!

Then, suddenly, she was there.

The first thing Mi did was turn out the light. "It isn't dark yet," she said.

Matthew watched her put two meagre spoonfuls of tea into the pot, watched the back of her shoulders and watched her as she veered towards him, making for the kettle.

She's been crying, he thought.

Mum?

Nothing. Just a sigh as she turned towards the table, setting the teapot down on the trivet that always stood there, ready and waiting. Also, two cups and saucers.

Mi sat across from the window — the window facing west, the sunset filtered through the steam and the steam turned to frost on the narrow panes. She lighted a cigarette and pulled the ashtray closer.

"I guess I'm going to have to give up smoking," she said.

"Why?"

"Because ..." She turned to look at him and then away. "We haven't any money."

Matthew waited.

His mother was stony still. He could see where she had tried to wipe the tears away from under her eyes — something he would not have seen if it hadn't been for the sunset. The window might have been made of stained glass.

"I'm sorry," she said. "I shouldn't have said we haven't any money. It's just the way it feels."

Matthew wondered what was wrong.

"That man who was here," Mi said — and waited while she edited what she had to say next. "He's what you call a dealer." She tipped the ash from her cigarette and poured them each a cup of tea while she spoke — speaking the way Miss Bransby spoke when she was explaining how to solve a problem in arithmetic — toneless, but precise.

"I'm having to sell a few things. You mustn't be upset. They're things we hardly ever use ..." Here, she smiled at him — unsuccessfully. "Some dishes. China. One or two pieces of silver."

"Have you told Dad?"

"No."

"Why not?"

"Because ... I don't want him to worry, being so far away and everything. I didn't want to tell you, either — but ..." She looked at him helplessly. "You came home so early. I thought you'd gone skating at Teddy's and ... I thought the man would leave before you got here. I'm sorry. I am sorry."

Matthew looked away, afraid she was going to cry again. Mi stood up.

"I'll go and call Bonnie," she said. "It's getting on to suppertime."

Before she left, she leaned down to kiss the top of Matthew's head.

"You're still wearing your toque," she said. And whipped it off and messed his hair. She actually laughed. "I thought I was bringing up a gentleman." Laying the toque on the table, she was gone.

Matthew sat there. He smoothed the oilcloth. The oilcloth was blue. Something was terribly wrong. What was it?

He waited.

Outside, it got dark.

In the morning, Mi told Matthew she was going away.

This had never happened before.

"For how long?" he asked.

"I don't know. Maybe a month."

"But it's Christmas. Dad may come home."

"No. He won't. He isn't coming home — so I'm going to him."

"To Halifax?"

"Yes."

"That's why you sold those things. To buy the ticket."

"Yes. It's very expensive. And ... I'll have to stay in a hotel."

"Are we going with you?"

"No."

Matthew said nothing.

Mi put another piece of toast in front of him.

"Eat your breakfast."

Matthew sat on his hands. He was wearing his new breeks with a cold leather seat and leather knees. "I'm not hungry," he said.

"Yes you are. Eat."

Mi was pouring milk on Bonnie's Red River Cereal.

Matthew said: "where will *we* go?"

"I haven't decided."

"*Mum.*"

"I haven't decided."

Mi drank tea.

"One whole month," said Matthew. "Come on, Mum. It's Christmas."

"Matthew — I am going to Halifax. I can't take you out of school and I can't cart Bonnie halfway across the country."

Matthew had almost lost his voice. "We never had Christmas alone before," he whispered.

"You won't be alone. You'll be with family, wherever you go."

"I want to go with you."

"Matthew. No."

"I WANT TO SEE DAD!"

Matthew had yelled this, not knowing it would come out that way.

Mi just stared at him. Then away, and then back again. "Hon," she said, "do you remember: *it was the best of times, it was the worst of times* ...?"

He nodded. "*Tale of Two Cities.*"

Mi said: "*it was the season of light, it was the season of darkness* ... yes?"

Now she leaned along the oilcloth towards him and pushed his hair away from his eyes. "*It was the spring of hope,*" she said. "*It was the winter of despair. We had everything before us and* ... what?" She waited. "Tell me. How does it end?"

"*We had nothing before us.*"

"Right. And what happened?"

Matthew was not sure how to answer. Then he said: "the French Revolution happened. Everybody died."

Mi said: "no, they didn't. Some of them survived. That's why we read it. They had to learn how to do that — how to survive in the worst conditions. They did. And that's what we're going to do."

She sat back.

"Eat your breakfast."

The guillotine fell. Another head rolled into the basket. Everybody cheered.

Bonnie said: "it's snowing. We can make a snowman."

In the dining-room, Matthew counted over what was missing. Sold. All the green Spode was gone — his favourite dishes, with peacocks strutting between the green rims. Also the candlesticks with crystal pendants and a silver mantle big enough to cover the Christmas turkey and a set of eight ruby glasses. *I've had to sell a few things*, his mother had said — but these were joys and wonders, each of them tagged with memories of other times — other, better times than these. Matthew stared at what remained in the china cabinet. Ordinary things. Not magical. Except for one lone figure — Pierrot, black and white in Meissen. Matthew took him down and hid him where his mother would not find him — in a box filled with tissue paper, set high up in his cupboard. On the lid, he wrote down: *NOT FOR SALE*. Some things have to stay the same.

This was December. 1940.

7th January, 1941

One week after New Year's — on a Tuesday — Mi arrived at
Ellen's in a taxi. Bonnie was in the back seat with Bear — Bear in
a brown paper bag.

Mi said: "is he ready?" meaning Matthew.

Ellen said: "yes. You're late."

The train from Montreal had been late. All the trains were late,
because of the war. *Because of the war. Because of the war.* Everything
was breaking down or broken *because of the war.* The train from
Halifax to Saint John was late. The train from Saint John to
Montreal was late. The train from Montreal to Toronto was late.
"IT'S NOT MY FAULT!" Mi said. "I'VE BEEN RUNNING
ALL THE WAY HOME!" She was wearing a blue coat.

Ellen said: "go and sit down in the living-room."

Mi went.

Isabel was in the dining-room, sorting afghan squares that she
and Ellen had crocheted to send to England. She glanced at Mi and
said: "you look dead."

"I am dead." And then: "aren't you going to welcome me
home?"

"Welcome home."

"Thank you."

Ellen came back from the kitchen and handed Mi a glass of
whisky.

"Drink this."

"Bonnie's waiting in the taxi. I can't be long."

"Drink it."

34

Mi sipped. Bonnie had stayed with Lewis and Loretta, Matthew with Isabel and Ellen. Now, they would be together again.

Ellen sat down on the edge of a chair.

"So?"

Mi took another sip. Larger.

"Can Matthew hear?"

"No. He's in the bathroom."

Mi stared at the floor. Then at her hand, with its glass of whisky.

"It's never been so bad," she said. "There's a good chance they'll let him go. Discharge him."

"A dishonourable discharge?"

"I suppose it would be. Yes."

Ellen pulled herself up to her feet and drank from a glass she had brought for herself.

"Alcohol turns him into a madman," she said. "It always did."

"Thanks for the brand-new information," said Mi.

Ellen looked at her.

"Michael," she said. "You and I are not at war. We're trying to save the same life."

Mi lifted her head, astonished. "I thought you hated him."

Ellen glanced at the mantel. "He's my son," she said. "I may not like him, but I will never hate him."

Mi looked away. "I shouldn't have said that."

"You're tired."

"Yes."

"Is there more?"

"How do you mean?"

"About Graeme. Is there more?"

Isabel came and stood in the doorway, an afghan square in her hand. It was green.

Mi said: "no." And then she burst into tears.

When Isabel stepped forward, Ellen waved her aside. Then she went and stood in the window with her back to the room.

They waited.

Mi set her glass on the games table beside her and blew her nose. After this, she took a long pull on the whisky and gave a wry laugh. "I suppose that tells you everything," she said. "Bursting into tears like that."

Ellen did not turn. When she spoke, it was not harshly. There was even kindness in her voice.

"You were not the first of his women," she said. "And you certainly won't be his last." Then she did turn and look at Mi. "The only good thing," she said, "is that they will tire of him. And you won't."

Mi did not reply. But she was thinking: *no. However crazy it may seem, I won't.*

Matthew came downstairs and stopped by the door. He looked like a refugee — like one of those photographs in the papers of children whose destination is uncertain.

Mi finished her drink and stood up.

"Hi, hon."

"Mum."

"Let's go home. Okay?"

"Yes."

"It's good to see you."

"Yes."

Oddly, they did not kiss. They did not even touch. Mi shook Ellen's hand and waved at Isabel, who waved back. Nothing more was said. They left.

At Crescent Road, Mi did not unpack. It was as if she intended to get right back on the train and leave them again. She put her suitcase in the front-hall closet and said: *you aren't to touch that.* As if they would.

Matthew kept an eye on it for the next few days until, on the Saturday, the suitcase was gone and he found it emptied in his mother's cupboard.

After that, Mi stayed at home and nothing more was said about going away.

In all this time, Graeme did not write once to the children. Now, he did not communicate with Mi. There was just a long, unbroken silence, as if his whereabouts were a classified secret. Censored. Then — in March — Matthew found an official-looking envelope in Mi's top drawer. It had been folded over and laid amongst her lingerie bags.

Someone, whose name meant nothing to Matthew, had written to say that *Flying Officer Matthew Graeme Forbes has been demoted to the rank of Pilot Officer and the Government allowance allotted to Mrs Forbes as the wife of a Royal Canadian Air Force officer will be downgraded accordingly.*

Matthew folded the letter into its envelope and put it back amongst his mother's things.

Demoted.

But Matthew was never told this in so many words — and Bonnie never knew. Mi never mentioned it. She sold some more china and considered selling the stones in her engagement ring. This, it turned out, she did not have to do until another year had passed. Then, she also sold her pearls.

12th July, 1941

Towards the end of May, Graeme was posted to Camp Borden, near Barrie, Ontario. Just over a month later, Mi went up to visit him. Matthew stayed with Isabel. Ellen went away to a friend's cottage in Muskoka. Bonnie was yet again with Lewis and Loretta. These arrangements were accepted in silence. Nothing was said about the children seeing their father. Mi suspected they had formed a pact. *We will not complain. Complaint is useless.* She was proud of them — and grateful. *My two little stoics.* She also knew this was a lie.

She was driven up to Barrie by Eloise Best. Eloise, whose husband, Roy, was a flying instructor at Camp Borden, had been there before and knew of some roadside cabins they could rent on the outskirts of town.

"Just so long as they haven't been named for the Seven Dwarfs," Mi said. "I can't stand cute."

"Don't worry," Eloise had told her. "These cabins are positively sedate. The woman who owns them looks as if she came down with Moses from the mountain top. You'll love them. Very Christian — very simple — very clean. The only drawback is the mottos hung on the walls."

"Mottos?"

"You know — *God Is Love* and stuff like that. She's pretty hot on spreading the word. Last time we were there, the motto over our bed was: *Thou Shalt Not Covet Thy Neighbour's Wife!*"

Mi roared. "Hah!"

Eloise, who was driving, said: "we had hysterics, too. Roy said: *do you think she minds if I covet my own wife?* In the end, we hid the

38

motto under the bed. The best damn weekend we've had in eight years."

Mi said: "you've only been married for seven."

"Well ..." Eloise turned and grinned. "We are young but once, my dear." Then she said: "didn't you and Graeme fool around before you were married?"

Mi did not know what to say. Certainly, Graeme had fooled around — with practically everything in skirts.

"Not with each other," she said. The truth was, there hadn't been any serious sex in her life before Graeme — and then, not until the honeymoon.

"You like it?" said Eloise, sounding perhaps a bit too inquisitive. "I mean, it's interesting to know how other people react. I wasn't asking for details, Mi."

Mi and Eloise had met when they were members of the Junior League. They had known each other for longer than Mi could remember. Eloise was five years younger, but that hardly seemed to matter. What they shared was an attitude to survival. They were both the children of troubled marriages, though only Mi's parents had been divorced. Eloise's father had killed himself over financial problems, but not before he had dragged his wife and children through hell. This way, Eloise understood what Mi went through with Graeme. It was implicit — and rarely a topic of conversation.

"So?"

Mi looked away.

Eloise went on. "Roy and I have a great time. Wonderful. Funny — exciting. And perilous ..."

"*Perilous?*"

"Oh, sure! Sometimes we hang from the chandelier. If we can find one. And sometimes ..." Eloise lowered her voice and swung the car out wide into the other lane. "Sometimes we do it standing on our heads."

"You're going to kill us, Eloise."

"Funny. That's what Roy always says."

Mi sat silent. Imperilled. "Please don't do that again."

Eloise waited. "There's nobody else on the road, Mi. Otherwise, I wouldn't have done it." And a minute later: "you still haven't told me."

"There isn't anything to tell." Mi got out her sunglasses and put them on.

Eloise gave up. "Okay. Let's play *I-spy-with-my-little-eye.*"

"Oh, for God's sake, El. We're not children."

Eloise glanced at her.

"Sorry," she said. "I guess I'd better shut up." But she was thinking: *I spy with my little eye the saddest kid on the block.*

The cabins were just as Eloise had described them: *positively sedate.* Each one had its own front porch and there were shutters on all the windows. They looked almost like grown-up playhouses — every detail a serious attempt to persuade the renter that God was in His Heaven and all was right with the world.

And all was right. When Graeme arrived, it was clear at a glance he had kept his word and had not been drinking. His eyes were alive and bright and the clouded look Mi had dreaded was gone. He smelled like a child — his hair, his hands, the back of his neck. And his uniform was pressed and all his buttons polished until they were blinding.

"Hello."

"Hello."

They stood there, silent under the trees with their fingers entwined and Mi's eyes filling with tears.

"I'm so proud of you," she said.

"Thank you."

"Please don't move for a moment. One day, this is going to make a splendid memory."

Graeme said nothing.

Then they went inside.

13th July, 1941

On the Sunday, there was a heat wave. Matthew made a fan for Isabel out of some cardboard and he also made her some lemonade. She was odd, today — not her usual talkative, sometimes funny self. Her hair was damp. It clung to her scalp, and a kind of hardness had taken hold of her mouth.

Around two-thirty, Matthew was ensconced reading — shirtless in his khaki shorts, leaning back in the sofa. Isabel was sitting in Ellen's chair, a usurper — dabbing her neck from time to time with a cotton handkerchief and fanning herself with the cardboard. Ice chips were melting in both their glasses.

Somewhere, a fly was buzzing — wanting either in or out. All the shades were drawn against the heat and it was hard to tell which side of the screen it was on.

Buzz-buzz.

Matthew stood up and moved to the window.

"You leaving me?"

"No. Just looking for that fly."

"Which fly?"

Buzz-buzz.

"That one."

"Leave him be. I don't want any killing here."

Matthew walked across to the hearth and ran his finger along the mantel. There were all the photographs of all the dead. Uncle Ian. Others. Grandfather Forbes.

"Where's the watch fob now?"

"Mother has it. Up on her vanity. He was her husband, after all. She got to keep all his mementos."

"What's a memento?"

"Something you have to remind you."

"What of?"

"Another person. Happy occasions. Other times."

Buzz-buzz.

"That damn fly."

"You aren't supposed to say that."

"Mother says it," said Matthew. "She says damn a lot."

"She's an adult." Typical Isabel. Not just an answer — an explanation.

The room fell silent. And then: "how come you never married?"

Nothing. Not even movement. Matthew looked at the cover of his book — open — splayed on the sofa. *Wuth-er-ing Heights.*

Finally: "the only man I ever loved died in 1917."

The war again. The other one.

"Just around this time of year. July. High summer." Her voice drifted off.

"Was he a hero? Like Uncle Ian?"

"In his way, yes. Very much so."

Isabel spoke without inflection, her head pressed back, eyes closed, her posture on a tilt — but frozen. She was, after all, sitting in Ellen's chair.

"What was his name?"

Father.

Isabel almost said it. Then she said: "is there any more lemonade?"

Matthew turned away from the mantel and took her glass.

"Please," she said. "But no more ice. It gives me a headache."

Around the time that Matthew went for the second serving of lemonade, Mi and Graeme were seated on the grass in front of their cabin.

Mi had spread a blanket for them to sit on. "You mustn't get grass stains on your uniform," she said — and smiled. "People will talk."

"Let them."

Graeme lay back with his arms behind his head.

Mi watched him.

Halfway through the night, he had left her. Lying in the moonlight, making love, she'd felt him leaving. His rhythm had changed. It was odd. Suddenly, they were not together. She was with him, but he was off with someone else.

Mi wondered what her name might be this time, and who she was. Up to now, of those she had known, the names had all been melodramatic: Alexandra! Moira! Eliza! The last, in Halifax, being Tatiana — breast-beating names that conjured women in sable hats and upturned collars, wearing nothing beneath their furs but lingerie — dark silk stockings — garter-belts ... Names all ending with exhalations — sighs and murmurs. Boy dreams of women — little to do with men. It was ridiculous. Before the war, when

Graeme was just another handsome man in a suit downtown, all of his women had names like Glad and Daisy — Lou and Betty — dime-store, lunch-counter names that conjured life-worn women whose only desire was to get off their feet and have someone buy them a drink and pay attention.

Well — *I WANT ATTENTION!*

Jesus.

Had she spoken?

No.

Should she?

What would she say? How would she put it?

Graeme — I know it's begun again — the women, if not the drink ... I suppose she works somewhere like this — changing the sheets and pillow cases, knowing who's been lying there — which of them are married — which of them are not ...

We're married.

Some roadside maid in a cheap hotel — some waitress in an overlit canteen ...

"Please don't stare at me, Mi."

Mi was silent.

Graeme said: "you mustn't spy on me. I'm doing my damnedest here. I'm doing my god-damned damnedest."

"I know that."

"All I want is ..."

Everything.

Graeme sighed.

"You want a cigarette?"

"Sure."

She lighted it for him and passed it down to his fingers. Then she lighted one for herself.

"Once they know I'm serious, I'm sure they'll give me a break," he said. "I'm really doing well. Really well. Really. Everyone says so. *A born administrator.*"

Mi wasn't deaf. She heard the bitterness. He would "fly a desk" till the end of the war, when all he'd wanted was to fly a plane. Like Roy. Like Ian. Heroes. The company of heroes. Aces. Men.

Not men, my darling. Boys. Just a boy. Ian was only nineteen. And you aren't a boy any more.

"I went up the other day," he said — his voice drifting back to her. "I've been up three times, now. *Part of my job, you see. Part of my job. The man behind the desk has to know what the man behind the controls is doing.* Roy takes me. The flights are great. Harvards. Yellow. Training planes. Built like a brick ..."

"Graeme!"

"Well, it's true. They gotta be sturdy. The students throw them around in the air like toys."

"Does Roy?"

"Not with me aboard, he doesn't."

Mi laughed.

She watched the top of his head. He was up in the air above them — Graeme looking down at everything, banking the plane and roaring into a dive.

Still the honeyed hair and still the shoulders of a quarterback. Still the expressive piano player's hands — their fingers splayed and thin, bony wrists that still could pull another man's hand to the table top in seconds. Five seconds — flat. She'd seen it. There he lay — Graeme — sky-dreaming — gone from her — just as he'd left her in the night — banking the plane and changing its rhythm.

Don't, my darling. Please don't crash.

Mi looked up. A shadow had fallen over her shoulders into her lap.

"Mrs Forbes?"

Mi turned and shaded her eyes.

It was the religious woman in all her Sunday blacks and greys
— the cabin owner. Moses' partner.

"Yes?"

"There's a phone call for you. Come with me."

Madame Evangeline marched away across the grass towards her
unpainted house, which also served as her office.

Mi stood up and started after her.

"I'll be right back," she said. "It's probably Loretta telling me
Bonnie won't eat her supper. Don't go 'way."

Graeme went on flying.

Mi did not come back for half an hour. When she did, he was
sound asleep.

Five o'clock, Sunday afternoon, the thirteenth of July, 1941.

Both the Bensons were lying down — Lewis on the living-room
sofa, Loretta on her bed upstairs.

In spite of civic pleas to conserve electricity, Lewis had plugged
in the fan and turned it on. It riffled what remained of his hair and
stirred the pages of his magazine — the magazine resting open on
his belly. *Liberty*. Five cents a copy.

Bonnie, who was hungry, came and stood in the doorway,
watching. Lewis had left her doing a jigsaw puzzle on the front
porch. Now, it was completed. A mountain in Switzerland. With
snow. The fan beside Lewis reminded her of an aeroplane propeller. Any minute, he would take off and head for the skies.
Maybe crash against the mountain on the front porch.

Bonnie gave her sun-dress a hitch. Its shoulders were loose and it had no belt and felt as if it was going to fall around her knees. She hated it, but that's what Loretta had dressed her in that morning. *It's light and airy, darlin' — perfec' dressin' for a day of heat wave.* Loretta's speech was more than somewhat affected by the fact that she was born in the state of Mississippi.

Lewis had *found her* in a hotel lobby down in Hattiesburg, south of Laurel. This was how their meeting was always described. *Heat! I thought I would die,* Lewis would say. *Dogs were dyin' in the streets,* Loretta always added. *Layin' right down in the gutters to expire!*

I had gone south on a mission for the T. Eaton Company, here in Toronto — this was Lewis — *in the year 1926 ...*

Scoutin' for cottons, he was. Loretta.

Tupelo — Winona — Yazoo — Vicksburg — Jackson — Laurel — Hattiesburg ...

Straight on down to the Delta. That's where he was makin'.

The names and destination were always given in the manner of a station-master sending off a train. Lewis and Loretta spoke their story hand over hand, all the sentences looping and locking like a two-handed braid — and their meeting was the bow with which the braid was tied.

By the time I got to Hattiesburg and the lobby of that hotel ...

... the Madison Hotel. On Water Street ...

... I was all set to drop. But there she was ...

... there I was ...

... all got up in white — cool as a dozen cucumbers — standing over by a bunch of flowers they'd put out to decorate the place. And I took one look ...

... that's all it took ...

... and I said to myself: that lady there is going to be my wife.

And so I was. And am.

Now, it was almost fifteen years to the day when they had met. Lewis Benson was Graeme's cousin on his mother's side and had recently succumbed to diabetes — now in the process of killing him. Or so it felt. And, if he died, nothing would be left of him. *Died without issue.* That's what the registry would say. Loretta had been afraid of giving birth. This way, they were childless. Not that it mattered deeply. They had other people's children — Matthew and Bonnie among them.

Was Lewis asleep? Yes. Bonnie could tell by his breathing — deep and heavy.

A chocolate bar would be nice. A box of them was kept above the sink for Lewis's episodes of diabetic crisis. Chocolate bars and bananas. Bonnie knew exactly where they were.

The kitchen was behind her, through a swinging door. Turning towards it, Bonnie was wondering whether Lewis and Loretta counted over the chocolate bars at the end of every day. (The bananas were of no interest.) At home, her mother always counted over the change in her purse before she went to bed. Bonnie could hear her doing this every night and the numbers being muttered aloud.

The door fanned the air. The momentary breeze was cool on the backs of Bonnie's legs.

Why is it so dark in here?

Only two windows, and the shades pulled tight.

Bonnie liked the smell of kitchens. Leftover toast and coffee smells — brown sugar, maple syrup — comfort smells. And chocolate.

Right above the sink, in a box, in a cupboard — Hershey bars.

Bonnie brought a chair and clambered up. The edge of the sink was cool against her bare knees. The smell of tap water also appealed. There was a glass right there for drinking purposes, and if she ran the tap and set the glass in the sink, the water would be icy cold by the time she had found her chocolate bar.

If only she could see.

She pulled the cupboard open past her face and leaned around the door. The light switch was down there somewhere. Her dress kept getting in the way.

To steady herself, she placed her right hand on the faucet — the faucet already sweating cold — and reached along the wall.

Where? Where?

There.

There.

In the living-room, the fan stopped turning.

Loretta came down the stairs in her shift.

"Lew, honey?"

Lewis stirred. *Liberty* fell to the floor.

"What time is it?"

"Near four-thirty, darlin'. Gettin' on to five. I can't make the lights work, honey. I figure maybe the heat wave has done in the fuse box. You think you're 'wake enough to go downstairs an' see? I'll put a kettle on — thank God for gas — and we can have some nice iced tea in those long, cool glasses we bought last Friday."

Loretta made for the kitchen. Lewis was struggling to his feet and when she suddenly shouted his name, he fell back, dizzy.

"Don't go yelling at me, 'Retta," he said. "I haven't got the strength."

Loretta, of course, didn't hear him. She was using the broom, trying to break Bonnie's grip on the faucet. By the time he got there, the child was lying dead on the floor.

Bonnie Michael Forbes. Seven. Of an accident. In the city of Toronto.

"Graeme?"

His head had turned to one side and his arms had fallen wide of his shoulders — winglike — unfeathered. His shirt was a pale shade of khaki, dampened darker by perspiration. His mouth was open.

Mi stood above him — silent.

Way, way off, she could hear an aeroplane approaching. In one of the cabins, someone had turned on a radio. A car drove by. Then a motorcycle. Then another car.

Graeme? I have something to tell you ...

Out on the lake, there was a sailboat, its canvas hanging loose, quivering in the negligent breeze.

Graeme?

Mi closed her eyes. And opened them. She sank in slow motion to her knees.

Above her, the fir trees stirred. There were birds. Wings. Calling.

"Graeme. Wake up."

He rolled away, withdrawing the arm whose hand had brushed against her skirt as she fell.

She heard him begin to sleep again — one long, sighing breath and the sound of parting lips.

Eloise came and found Mi bowing there — folded over against her knees, with her hands locked tight across the back of her neck.

"Darling? What is it?"

For a moment, there was no response and then Mi's hands unlocked and fell to the ground as fists.

"Get me up," she said.

Eloise bent in over Mi's back and lifted her by the elbows.

"Hold me."

"Yes. Yes. It's all right."

Mi looked down at Graeme.

"Isn't he beautiful," she said.

Eloise said nothing. She held Mi tighter.

Then Mi broke away and walked across the lawn to her cabin steps.

Eloise followed and when she got there, Mi said: "give me a cigarette."

Eloise did this — took one herself and lighted them both.

Roy came out on their cabin porch and said: "you coming back?" He was shirtless and wore a towel around his neck.

Eloise waved him off.

"Is something wrong?"

"I'll be there in a minute."

Roy went back inside.

Mi smoked her cigarette and stared at space. Everything around her seemed to be waving *goodbye* — the sails on the lake — the tops of the trees — the birds in the sky. She reached out for Eloise and held her hand so hard that Eloise was alarmed.

"Tell me."

Mi took a gulp of air.

"Bonnie," she said, looking past her friend at Graeme. The rest could not be put into words. *Bonnie*. That was all.

Two hours later, Roy walked Eloise over to their car, his red hair darkened with shower water. He put her suitcase into the trunk and took her hand.

"Don't worry," he said. "I'll take care of him. You take care of her."

"Don't let him start again," said Eloise.

"I'll do my best."

"A Best can't do better," she said. It was their family joke. But this time, it was just an automatic response. She didn't smile.

They both turned to watch as Mi and Graeme crossed the grass. In the dying light, the cabins and the trees behind them looked like an etching. Graeme was pale as a piece of paper. His eyes had died. Mi was expressionless.

At the car, she turned to him and said, without looking at him: "goodbye."

"Goodbye."

Eloise kissed him. "We'll phone," she said, "as soon as we know what happens next." And then to Roy: "goodbye, my darling."

Mi looked back as the car pulled away and watched as Roy and her husband disappeared.

Two days later, Bonnie was buried. In a box that might have held two dozen long-stemmed roses. So it appeared. Roy said later to Eloise: *dead people look so small.* Holding Graeme's hand, Mi thought: *somehow, we have to get through this together — even though we're apart.* Half an hour later, he was gone — driven back to Borden with Roy beside him in an official R.C.A.F. vehicle. Everyone saluted. No one had a name. It was a nightmare of anonymity. Even Roy was faceless. Even Graeme. They returned — were returning — to the world where men and women were just statistics — numbers dressed in blue or khaki. A child had died, but whose would not be said. Her name was folded over and returned to Graeme's file: *C2425*. Sifting into place, it barely made a sound. Then, silence — followed by the banging of the filing cabinet drawer.

Now, the grave can be explained and its picture set aside: a certainty. We know now whose it is and what it portends in terms of those whose flowers are set out at its foot. To be haunted by the memory of a child. Not to have said goodbye. *Not to have held her one last time. If only: these are the words you will live with forever. If only I had. If only I hadn't. If only. But in the photographs, she is still alive. In the photographs, with Bear, she is life itself.*

16th July, 1941

Reveille would be at six.

On the morning after Bonnie's funeral, Graeme woke at five and could not get back to sleep. Sleep, at best, had been fitful all through the night and he'd spent a lot of time on the john — smoking cigarettes and staring into space.

The lights, he wrote — would write — to Michael, *in this godforsaken bathroom are pure white hell — glaring down at me from the ceiling — blinding me from above the sink. Finally, I turned them off and sat in the dark. When Symons, my room-mate, got up to take a midnight leak, he had a pretty bad shock, stumbling into my knees!*

A pretty bad shock.

What could Bonnie possibly have felt? Known. *Felt.* No time for fear, that was certain. No time to know, thank God, what was happening to her. Only being shaken through and through by a force that meant nothing to her. It turned on the lights, that's all.

Or turned them off.

Terminated. Bonnie. Born May 25, 1934 — died July 13, 1941.

Only seven years of days, Mi — two thousand, five hundred and fifty-five, if you round it out. Plus this year's days of June, the six last days in May that followed the 25th and the thirteen days of July through which she almost lived. Also one for the leap year that came just once in her life. Two thousand, six hundred and four.

Still, he would write, *for all the sadness I feel — for me and for her, nothing matches my sadness for you. You've lost three children, now — both the stillborn babies and Bonnie — and though I lost them, too, I didn't have to carry them — I didn't suffer their births — and I didn't endure the fear you must have felt (I know you did) that your body had somehow turned against you and was killing your children of its own free will.*

Two thousand, six hundred and four — and most of them, days she spent with you. Far more time than I had with her. Far, far more — and my fault entirely.

6:00 A.M. — and the distant sound of reveille.

I hate it here. I hate this bathroom — I hate the lights. I hate the deadly routine. I hate the room I sleep in and I hate the man who shares it with me. I hate the crowding and I hate the loneliness. And I hate, I hate, I hate above all the god-damned children, men and women, babies, dogs and cats and horses — everything that survived the last three days and woke to see this morning. And I hate ...

Here, Graeme's letter ended.

It was never sent. It was never written. He wrote it only in his mind, unable to confront such thoughts on paper. Unable to watch the words being formed — unable to write his name — unable to claim the sentiments implicit in his usual signature: *with all my love, yours only, Graeme.* They had always been a lie, but now he meant them and could not write them down.

When Symons awoke, he found Graeme sitting up in bed. Nothing was said.

Symons finished dressing himself and prepared to leave for the mess.

"Maybe you should come at least for a cup of coffee."

Graeme shook his head.

"I'm off, then."

Yes. But not a word aloud.

When Symons had gone, Graeme lay back on his pillows. *I'll wake up*, he thought, *and none of this will have happened.*

But it had and he knew it had and he didn't even close his eyes. He lay that way for the next two hours and after that he got up and went to his bureau. The photographs there were of his father, his brother, Ian, and of Mi together with the children. Graeme picked up the latter and removed it from its frame. Folding it, he made a breakable crease and tore away his daughter's image. Kissing it, he closed his eyes and tore it twice again and placed the pieces in an ashtray. Setting them on fire, he held the match until it burned him. Only then did he pinch it out. His finger and his thumb smelled of ash — of sulphur — and of flesh.

In the six months following Bonnie's death, their lives were turned entirely upside down. Just as the war was destroying more than a century of public certainties, so what had been accepted as private certainties — the roof above your head, the food on your plate, the clothes on your back — were all in jeopardy. Nothing, now — as someone said — would ever be the same.

Ellen, having watched him from her chair, decided that Matthew was in danger of an entirely female world and required a male environment to provide him with the resources Graeme was denying him — wilfully or not — by his absence. *School,* she said to Mi one Sunday. *A boarding school, where other boys and men can offer what is missing from his life.*

Of course, there was only one acceptable school: *St Andrew's College*, where Ian had gone. And Graeme, too. A school that Tom had endowed. A school where academic honours had rained on Ian's head and, though it was incidental, Graeme had been an athletic star. *And I will pay*, she said. *I insist. Matthew is now all we have of the future.*

There was more.

Lewis and Loretta — due to one of Lewis's endless miscalculations — had lost their house and required — if only temporary — haven. "They can't come here," said Ellen. "There isn't room. Besides which, I could not abide her presence. Loretta, for all her pretensions, is an ignoramus. She thinks — good heavens — that we are all *Americans* and cannot understand the difference between us. I wonder who she thinks we are."

Mi had to smile. Ellen was so rarely animated, but the subject of Loretta's social pretensions brought her entirely to life. Or, perhaps, it was the sherry.

"What I propose," Ellen continued, "is that you will come and live here with us. There is, after all, enough room for that. And when Matthew comes on holidays, he can sleep in Graeme's old room. This will not only save you paying rent, but it will put a little cash in your pocket."

"I'm afraid I don't quite understand," Mi said.

"They, dear — Lewis and Loretta — will go and live in your house. Pay the rent and you will come here."

Mi stared.

"I don't want to leave my house. I love it. It's my home."

"Which you cannot afford."

Mi looked away.

Ellen said: "you cannot afford it, Michael. And, with Matthew at school and Graeme in the Air Force and ..."

... with Bonnie dead ...

"... you would be entirely alone."

Perhaps I want to be entirely alone.

Mi looked at the mantelpiece. Where was Bonnie? She belonged up there.

The clock ticked.

"Reality," said Ellen. "I'm sorry, Michael — but it's where we have to live."

Yes.

We have to live.

So be it. She would live with Ellen, and Isabel would hover over her shoulder. Three women. One boy. And an absent husband. *The New World Order.* Wasn't it called that? Or something.

The day was cool and blue, with piles of September clouds on the horizon. Eloise drove them up Yonge Street, down the long slow drop of Hogg's Hollow, up the other side in a race with the Radial Car, under the trees of Thornhill, climbing, climbing all the way to Aurora.

"I don't see any school."

"You will."

Matthew was in the back seat, Mi up front with Eloise.

"I want to go home."

Mi ignored this. "It's on the far side of town, on the left."

Eloise said: "there's a drugstore and soda fountain up ahead. Anybody interested?"

"Sure. We're in lots of time."

They sat on high-legged stools in front of the counter. The counter was grey and shiny. It smelled of bleach. Eloise had a chocolate soda. Mi had a cup of coffee. Matthew had a Coke.

Above him, a fan was spinning. Whirring — whirling. If Matthew stood on his stool, his neck would be just the right height for the metal blades to strike off his head. It would fall to the floor at his mother's feet. Then she'd be sorry ...

"Aren't you going to finish your Coke?"

Matthew didn't answer. He used his elbow to shunt the glass away.

"Well, I guess we'd better be pushing off," said Eloise. "This isn't getting us anywhere." She stubbed her cigarette and started moving towards the front of the store. Mi followed.

At the door, they turned back.

Matthew was still seated.

Looking at him, Eloise said: "you'd think we were sending him to the electric chair."

Mi stiffened.

Eloise suddenly realized what she had said. "I'm sorry. That was thoughtless."

"Yes, it was. But never mind."

Mi hung there, wavering, lost, not knowing which way to go. Then she pushed at the screen door and went out onto the sidewalk. "You get him," she said to Eloise. "I can't drag him after me any more."

She went to the curb and blindly crossed the street, not quite knowing what she was doing. A truck went by behind her, moving so fast she felt the draught of its passage lifting her skirts. At the car, she got in without waiting for the others. Two miscarriages. *One dead daughter. Now this. I've lost all my children*.

She slammed the door.

When Matthew and Eloise crossed the road, Matthew was carrying a parcel.

Sliding in behind the wheel, Eloise said: "I bought him a box of chocolates."

Mi could see him in the rear-view mirror. Her son, in blue blazer, grey flannel shorts and school cap, holding a brown paper bag. He was staring grimly out at the street, his head turned to one side, his mouth set. She had seen him this way so many times — on all those streetcar journeys to Ellen's or the Bensons'. Why had she done it to him? To them both. Dragging them around like dolls and leaving them as if forgotten. She closed her eyes. *Dear God — the things we do to one another*.

St Andrew's College sits at the top of a hill, overlooking its playing fields below. Once through the gates, the approach leads up a wide, curving drive, debouching under trees into the quad.

A temporary sign made of cardboard directed them to one of the red-brick buildings on the right. Macdonald House.

In the hallway, a woman dressed entirely in white stepped forward and introduced herself as Mrs Hodges. "I'm Matron," she said. "I will show Forbes where he sleeps."

Turning left at the top of the stairs, they passed along a darkened corridor, while Mrs Hodges explained that the lights would not go on until dusk. "The war, don't you know. Every bit helps. So we're told." She pointed out the latrines, the shower room, the Floor Master's room, the head prefect's room. All the doors were closed, and gave the impression of being locked. Finally, Mrs Hodges came to one that seemed to be isolated from the rest.

"Here we are, then."

She gave the door a dramatic push and light gushed into the corridor, almost blinding them.

Mrs Hodges urged them forward. Matthew went first and the others followed.

Twelve beds and six windows. Twelve cupboards and twelve chairs. Twelve lamps — three overhead fixtures — and the door.

Mrs Hodges went and stood by one of the beds that faced the windows.

"This will be you, Forbes."

"Where are all the others?" Mi wanted to know, the room being empty.

"Most of them don't arrive until tomorrow. Old boys. Only the new boys arrive today. There will be one other in here with Forbes. He arrives this evening."

"Good." Mi turned to Matthew. "Well, it seems very pleasant."

"Yes," said Eloise.

Matthew said nothing.

Mrs Hodges said: "Forbes takes the cupboard to the left as he faces the bed. There are drawers for shirts and underwear, socks, et cetera. A shelf below for shoes, a shelf above for personal items. So. I will leave you now. Arrivals, arrivals." Bustle, bustle. Starch and corsets. Jangling keys and leather heels. They could hear her progress all the way along the corridor and down the stairs.

Somewhere, a toilet was flushed.

Matthew sat on the bed. Cement.

"I'll help you unpack," said Mi.

"No, don't," said Matthew.

Mi glanced at Eloise, then back. She forced a smile. "All right," she said. "You want to say goodbye up here, or come with us to the car?"

"The car," said Matthew. He refused to look at either his mother or Eloise. Standing up, he led them from the room.

By the car, he said: "Mum, don't call me Mattie any more."

He still hadn't looked at her. She took his chin in her hand and forced him to raise his eyes. "I'll see you around," she said. Then she got in the car and closed the door.

From the top of the hill, he watched them curve away out of sight. Nobody waved. And then they were gone. He was alone.

The brown paper bag sat on his bed, up by his pillow. Matthew sat down and touched it with his finger.

Bonnie.

It was her memento.

Bonnie's brown paper bag of Bear — in memory of all their journeys on the streetcar. She had carried it with her everywhere.

Matt removed the box of chocolates and smoothed the bag and folded it and stared at it and kissed it and put it in his pocket. Then he lay back on the bed and waited, not knowing why or what for. Just waiting, that was all.

In August, Roy had been posted to Trenton Air Base and Graeme was left up at Borden with no one to watch over him, no one available to keep him away from the taps and switches of his endless search for consolation — women — drink — forgetfulness.

The first indication Mi had that things had begun to go wrong was something Eloise said.

"Roy's going to be lonely, with no one to pick up after."

"What does that mean?"

"It means I have a big mouth."

"What does it mean, Eloise?"

"Nothing." Eloise smiled. Then she put on her Rosalind Russell imp-from-hell expression and said: "you're Graeme's wife. You've seen him do it — dropping his underwear and socks the way Hansel and Gretel drop breadcrumbs. He's famous for it — you've told me yourself."

"No I haven't."

Eloise turned away.

"I couldn't possibly have told you that — because it isn't true. He's neat as a pin. In fact — HE PICKS UP AFTER ME!"

"Stop yelling." And then: "it's bad for your voice." And then: "so — he had a few. Main thing is, he's back to being a Flying Officer. He's not going to put that in jeopardy again." And then:

"if you don't believe me, Mi, phone Roy at Trenton and he'll tell you. It was only a momentary lapse. Just a lapse." And finally: "everybody has lapses. Be forgiving."

What? Forever?

Now, as October drew to a close, the rains abated and all up and down the streets people began to burn their leaves. It was a time of year Mi had always loved. As a child she had helped her brothers rake huge piles of fallen leaves — mountains of them — into which they would jump and hide. And all through October the mountains would multiply until there would be a whole range of them strung along the street in front of their house. *The Maple Leaf Mountains of Outremont.* And on Hallowe'en, all the fathers of Cornish Avenue would step out together and, on a signal, torch the leaves until the whole curving range was ablaze from end to end.

October.

Mattie was born October 30th.

Mattie. Matthew. Matt.

And ...

What? What else was good about October — besides its storms and births and fires?

This year, the Germans got almost as far as Moscow. And Roy went to Trenton. And I stopped receiving money from ...

That bastard up at Camp Borden.

The day before Mi's move to Foxbar Road was Hallowe'en. Eloise had phoned to say she would not be able to spend the evening answering the door with Mi because she would have to answer the door at home. Her mother had developed a migraine and was indisposed.

Such as they were, Mi kept the handouts in a wooden salad bowl near the door. That morning, she had gone over to Yonge Street to The Nifty Nook and bought a large bagful of penny candy. Licorice cigars and pipes, jelly babies, chocolate-covered marshmallow moons, orange envelopes of sherbet powder, jawbreakers and Rose Buds. Up at Adams's she bought some apples, a package of wooden skewers and half a pound of brown sugar. Mrs Adams wagged her finger: "there are shortages enough, Mrs Forbes. Don't you go wasting that sugar on Hallowe'en." She also went into Max's Flowers and bought a single rose — not knowing why, just thinking: *I want one.*

Now, the rose was in a silver bud vase sitting near her chair in the living-room and the candied apples she had made, despite Mrs Adams's warning, were set out like windfall on a tray beside the salad bowl.

She turned on all the lights and waited.

Why am I nervous?

Because you're alone.

It's not the first time.

No — but it's the first Hallowe'en.

True. Oh, God. I want my children.

There will be lots of children.

Yes, but not mine.

Vaguely, she wondered if all the children in heaven were dressing up tonight.

You don't believe in heaven.

Tough.

The doorbell started ringing. On and off it rang for more than an hour. *Boo* — a pirate. *Boo* — a ghost. *Boo* — a skeleton. *Boo* — a cat and *boo* — a flapper.

Soldiers with dirty faces, the King of Hearts and Popeye. All of the Seven Dwarfs — twice over, but no Snow White. Tramps in tatters, tin-pot knights and flour-bag clowns. Grown-up ladies smeared with their mothers' lipstick, wearing high-heeled shoes. Witches with broomsticks, paper cloaks and pointy hats; lily-white maids and charming princes; pumpkinheads and the Three Little Pigs.

Non-stop tricksters came and went until after eight o'clock, all of them smelling of leaf smoke, candied breath and mothballs.

When it was over, Mi still had a little bit of booty in the bottom of the bowl and a single candied apple on a stick. Who knows — there might yet be a goblin or two on the prowl and it wouldn't hurt to leave things out.

She bolted the door, put on the chain and went into the dining-room.

Now, it's my turn to get drunk.

Don't be ridiculous.

Why not? I've waited long enough. Why should he have all the fun, and me all the misery?

Michael!

Don't call me that. You sound like Mother.

Mi got an unopened bottle of Johnny Walker from the side-board and took it into the kitchen.

Hadn't you better eat something first?

I'll eat when I damn well please.

Suit yourself. But drinking on an empty stomach …

IS ONE OF THE WORLD'S GREATEST PLEASURES!

My, my, my. We are on a tear.

Fuck off.

I beg your pardon?

You heard me.

Where did you pick that up?

Graeme!

Mi was struggling with the stopper, pushing at it so hard she bruised her thumb. Once it was out, she took the tumbler from beside the sink and sat at the kitchen table.

"Please don't ring," she said to the doorbell — and poured two fingers of Scotch.

It burned, but it was good. It burned all the way past her tongue and down her throat and she closed her eyes to savour it. Once in her belly, the heat spread out towards her diaphragm and up beneath it to her heart. One deep breath and her shoulders fell. The back of her neck might just have received a massage.

The only problem was the dreaded overhead light.

Forget it.

She kicked off her shoes and poured more Scotch.

Who's looking, who's counting?

She also lighted the first of the evening's cigarettes.

What if Graeme crashes in one of these stupid flights
he insists on taking?

Good.

Smoke.

I'd be rid of him.

No, you wouldn't.

Yes, I would. I'd forget him, just like that.

The way you've forgotten Bonnie?

You ... absolute ... bastard.

Well?

You absolute ...

Doorbell.

Oh, don't.

"Don't," she said aloud. "Now, some poor child is going to see me drunk."

You aren't drunk.

I will be. If only the god-damned bell would stop

ringing.

"COMING!"

Mi set down the glass and stubbed her cigarette and went out into the hall. Leaning towards the vestibule, she could see the front door with its full-length panel of bevelled glass, but there was no one there.

Until the ringing started again.

Mi went into the vestibule and scanned the porch.

Eloise, wearing her raccoon coat and carrying a Simpson's shopping bag, was standing looking back along the walk.

"I thought you said you couldn't come. Your mother."

"I hit her on the head with a brick. Won't do the migraine much good, but it set me free."

Mi pointed to the Simpson's bag. "Are you here to trick-or-treat?"

"Not unless you happen to have a case of Scotch."

Mi blinked. "Come in."

Eloise swept past her, brushing Mi's arm with fur and a leather glove.

"You have many kids?"

"Thousands."

"Me, too. But when it started to slacken off, I thought to hell with it, I'm going to Mi's. Mother can handle the dribs and drabs."

"I thought you said you hit her with a brick."

"I did." Eloise reached down into the Simpson's bag. "Voila! One brick!"

It was a bottle of Scotch.

Mi burst out laughing.

"You got her drunk."

"Tiddly."

"Come with me."

Mi led the way to the kitchen. "See?" she said. "I can match you brick for brick."

Now it was Eloise's turn to laugh. She picked up Mi's Johnny Walker and said: "looks like I've got some catching up to do."

Half an hour later, each with her own bottle, each her own glass and each her own ashtray, they sat on either side of the dining-room table, "smoking" licorice cigars.

Eloise looked at the boxes and suitcases piled all along the walls. She toasted them with a fresh glass of Scotch and said: "what's Ellen going to say when she sees you arrive with all that?"

Mi took a sip of her drink. "What can she say? It was her idea." After a moment, she said: "I want to show you something — but only if you promise not to tell."

"Cross my heart and hope to outlive Mother."

Mi stood up and went to the boxes, bringing one of the smaller ones back to the table. Setting it down before Eloise, she said: "look at that."

NOT FOR SALE, Eloise read.

"Open it," said Mi.

Eloise lifted the lid. Tissue paper. She rummaged, finally pulling the Meissen Pierrot into the light. "Beautiful," she said. "But I don't understand."

Mi said: "Matthew."

"Matthew?"

"When I was selling all that stuff, Matthew took it and hid it in his cupboard. When I was packing, I found it." She reached out and touched the whitened face with its single black tear. "I'm going to put it in his room at Ellen's."

Eloise set the figure on the table. "Children," she said, "do the damnedest things."

"Yes," said Mi. "And the most wonderful."

Mi had brought the rose from the living-room and put it between them under the cut-glass chandelier. Now she put the Pierrot beside it.

"Where'd you get that?" said Eloise. "The rose."

"Graeme."

"Oh? I'm impressed. What's the occasion?"

"Does there have to be an occasion?"

"Maybe not." Eloise rolled her cigar between her lips. "Flowers, eh? I didn't know people did that any more."

"Well, these people do."

"Unh-hunh." There was a pause. Eloise poured Scotch. "Why'd he only send one?"

"Oh, for heaven's sake! Use your imagination."

"I don't have an imagination." Eloise flicked the end of her cigar and raised her eyebrows like Groucho Marx. "My parents didn't buy me one."

Mi looked down and set her cigar aside. Then she reached out and touched the rose with the end of her finger. "It's in memory of Bonnie," she said. "On All Souls' Eve. Isn't it beautiful." She smiled.

Eloise almost wept. "Yes," she said. "It is. Beautiful."

"There they are," Mi said. "My children." Pierrot and a rose. She drew back her hand and folded it around the glass. "I vote we get drunk."

"Aren't you drunk already?"

"No. I haven't felt a thing."

"Well. Bombs away!" Eloise emptied her glass.

Another silence fell between them.

Outside, a wind had risen and now it howled in the chimney.

"A few leftover ghosts," said Eloise.

"Only one," said Mi.

Silence again.

"Roy says we may lose the war."

"You trying to cheer me up?"

"No — just changing the subject."

"You *can't* change the subject. That's all there is — drunken, womanizing husbands, dead babies and war."

"You left out Bette Davis."

When Mi looked up, Eloise was stirring her Scotch with her finger, its red nail magnified through the glass. "And you *can't* leave out Bette Davis. She's the answer to all your problems — and all your prayers."

"Ho."

"She is, you know."

Mi drank and sat back in her chair.

"You see *The Little Foxes*?" said Eloise.

"Not yet, no. Can't afford it."

"Can't afford it? Come on, Mi — that's ridiculous. Can't afford to go to the movies?"

"Nope. Not until the Borden Bastard sends me some money."

"You've got to be kidding."

"Why would I kid about that?" Mi lighted a cigarette.

"You can afford to smoke," said Eloise. "You can afford to drink bricks. You eat, don't you? Isn't that a roof up there somewhere? Can't afford to go to the movies? B.S.!"

"I dare you to say that out loud."

"What?"

"B.S."

Eloise straightened, raised her glass and drew in her chin. Lifting one eyebrow, she looked at Mi and said: "Bean Soup."

Mi exploded with laughter.

"Not only Bean Soup, my dear," said Eloise, "but also Blue Skies, Belle Starr and Brown Sugar!"

Mi said: "Barbara Stanwyck!"

"Benito Sussmolini!"

Giggles.

"Bald Spot!"

"Blood Sucker!"

Eloise got to her feet and leaned across the table.

"Are you ready for it?"

Mi stood up.

"Yes!"

"All together! Everybody! One! Two! Three!"

"BULL SHIT!"

The rose fell over between them.

Mi blinked.

Eloise picked up the rose and put it back in the bud vase.

"Sorry," she said.

"Maybe we should eat," said Mi.

"Can't afford it," said Eloise, and poured more Scotch into their glasses. "After. Later. When we're rich, we'll eat. Right now, we're poor — so we'll drink."

They drank and listened to the wind.

Finally, Mi said: "how come Bette Davis is the answer to all my prayers?"

"In *The Little Foxes*, she kills her husband."

"That's not new. She must've killed twenty husbands."

"Not until *The Little Foxes*."

"In *The Letter*. She killed her husband in *The Letter*."

"In *The Letter* she killed her lover. Not the same thing. But — in *The Little Foxes*, she sits right there and lets him die. *Watches* him dying ... of a heart attack." Eloise sat up straight and made a Bette Davis mouth. "Go right ahead. Be my guest. *Die — die — die!*" Then she sat back. "It's heaven. We should all take lessons."

"I don't want to be Bette Davis."

"Oh? Then what's all this about the Borden Bastard?"

"I could kill him."

"There you are, then. Tomorrow, we'll go and see *The Little Foxes*. Find out how to do it."

"Please be serious."

"Who — me?" Eloise laughed. Then she looked across at Mi. "I am being serious," she said, and meant it. "What you need is a good dose of Bette Davis spunk. Tell the Borden Bastard to take his rose and go to hell. Tell him: *either you straighten up and fly right, or take a walk!*"

All of a sudden, Mi started to cry.

"Oh, for God's sake."

"He didn't send the rose," she said. And then: "I'm sorry."

"There you go again. Little Miss I-Never-Cry — when, damn it all, you should. But, no — whenever you do, you apologize. Jesus, Michael. If anybody has a right to cry ..."

"I hate crying. *I hate it!*"

"Keep your hat on."

"I'M NOT WEARING A GOD-DAMNED HAT!"

Later, up in the bedroom, Eloise helped Mi into the bed.

"You okay?"

"Yes, sir."

"Sleepy?"

"No, sir. Drunk."

"Well, more power to you."

In the bed, Mi turned away. "Pardon my back," she said. Eloise patted Mi's shoulder. *Dear Lord,* she thought. *Forgive us our sins.* And then: *so this is war.*

Mi slept.

Matthew met and liked a boy whose name was Rupert Wright. Rupert was pale and small and mysterious. His teeth protruded. His hair was almost white. He had enormous hands that seemed like weights designed to hold his arms in place. He rarely raised them higher than his waist — except to eat. When seated he would place his elbows on the table to support them.

Rupert was some kind of genius. This was Matthew's opinion. Also the opinion of several of the Masters. It was not, however, the opinion of most of the boys in their dormitory and class. He was mercilessly beaten by a boy called Marsden and shunned by virtually everyone but Matthew. When Marsden attacked him, he did so in the company of another boy who was known as *Dixie.* Dixon. Dixon held Rupert down while Marsden pummelled him. Seeing this, Matthew ran to stop it. Not that he was brave. He was simply outraged. He didn't even think what he was doing.

Rupert and Matthew would sit in contented silence — sharing the broken squares of a Mackintosh toffee or sipping a Pepsi from separate straws.

Rupert's mother was famous. Why she was famous was never mentioned. *She's famous, that's all*. Perhaps an actress. Or an heiress. Certainly wealthy. She always arrived in a large black car whose driver was uniformed. She was American. "We never live in houses," Rupert said. "We're always in hotels. Suites with sitting-rooms and bedrooms — all with their own bath-rooms. Mother puts flowers out everywhere we go. Great big bunches in great big vases. Sometimes they're waiting for us when we arrive."

"Are there ever other people?"

"No. Just us."

On a weekend, Matthew was allowed to take Rupert home with him to Ellen's house on Foxbar Road and they climbed over the high board fence and went down into the cemetery.

"Have you dead people?"

"Yes. My father."

"My sister died last summer."

"Is she in here?"

"No. But I come here all the time."

They moved amongst the graves.

"This is the *City of Benares*," said Matthew. "I counted."

They had talked about the *City of Benares*. Rupert's uncle had been on board — and survived. But the image of the ship going down, end up and plunging out of sight in twenty minutes, had been a part of their mutual nightmare. Matthew told Rupert they

were sailing on the *City of St Andrew's* — and must learn to survive its sinking.

"Why would it sink?"

"Because we're children."

Neither elaborated. They knew they were in peril. What more
need be said?

Standing beside a gravestone — where chrysanthemums had
been left the day before — Matthew looked out over all the rest
and said: "eighty-seven children. Two-hundred and six adults. I
counted. The very same number as here. And, every Sunday,
someone brings flowers."

Rupert said: "I hate chrysanthemums."

When Matthew looked at him, wondering, he saw that Rupert
had been cast adrift in sorrow.

He took Rupert's hand. Enormous. Bony. Sad.

Bonnie was dead. Rupert, alive.

You lose one. You gain one.

Matthew said: "cheese-and-bacon toasts."

Rupert said: "yes."

In a silver dish.

On a Sunday. December 7, 1941.

On Christmas day, they were alone. Entirely. Mi and Matthew.
Matthew and Mi.

There had been such a long tradition — stretching all the way
back into Ellen's childhood — of a grand parade down the stair-
case, through whatever hallways there were and into living-rooms
ablaze with a lighted tree, a lighted fireplace and chairs alight with
presents — each recipient having a separate, pre-allotted chair —

and all the stockings filled with oranges, walnuts, apples, tiny tin-foil toys, whistles, flutes, pecans — and candy hanging from the mantel.

Now, this year, not only Graeme and Bonnie were absent, but Ellen and Isabel as well. They were in Florida, having accepted an invitation from Palm Beach. Graeme had just been posted to Trenton, where at least he would have the companionship of Roy. Bonnie was plain gone. Forever.

At nine o'clock, Mi and Matthew stood at the top of the stairs, not sure how to proceed.

Matthew ran his finger along the balustrade.

"You want to go first?" Mi said.

"Okay."

She touched his shoulder.

"Hon?"

He turned. Mi was smiling. "Merry Christmas," she said. "Go on, then."

Matthew went down the stairs.

The fireplace was dark.

There wasn't any tree.

And in his chair, there was only a hockey stick, an envelope and a book.

In Mi's chair, there was nothing.

She stood behind him and watched.

"I hope the stick's the right size," she said.

It was.

The book was called *Two Little Savages* by Ernest Thompson Seton. All down the sides of most of the pages, there were draw-ings. Bows and arrows, animals, birds. There were also full-page illustrations. In the fly-leaf, Mi had written: *for my son, Matthew*

Forbes, on Christmas Day, 1941 — with all my love, from Mum.

He thanked her.

"Open the envelope."

Matthew, it said.

He lifted the flap.

Inside, there was a piece of paper folded around a ten-dollar bill. On the paper: *Matthew, with love from Dad.*

Written in Mi's undeniable hand.

"He wants you to buy some skates," she said.

"Thanks."

Matthew put the money in one pocket and the letter in another. Then he said: "yours is in the dining-room."

"A surprise?"

"I guess."

They went and stood in the doorway, looking through at the table.

On the table, there was a box done up with ribbon.

"It looks as if you've been to the Women's Bakery and bought a cherry pie."

Mi was beaming.

"No," said Matthew. "Guess again."

He was carrying the hockey stick and the book. He wore his navy blue sweater, grey flannel shorts, a white shirt. His hair would not lie down.

Mi kissed the top of his head. "You're full of static. Electricity."

He was smiling. Nervous. "Open your present."

"What *can* it be?"

Mi picked it up.

"Not too heavy," she said. "Not like any pie I ever heard of."

"Don't shake it. Don't."

"It's breakable?"

"Sort of. Be careful."

Mi undid the ribbon, the bow meticulous. *Matthew*. She smiled at him.

Inside the box, there was tissue paper. Inside the tissue paper, Mi felt the shape of something round and thin.

"A cake plate?"

"Nope." And then, again: "be careful."

Mi pulled the tissue away.

"A record! Hon! How lovely!"

"Look and see what it is."

Mi peered.

Oh.

She closed her eyes.

My Bonnie Lies Over the Ocean. Sung by Connie Boswell.

Neither of them spoke. Mi sat down.

Matthew was still in the doorway.

"You don't have to play it now," he said. "I just thought ..."

Mi looked away.

"I just thought," he said, "there ought to be something."

That was Thursday, December 25, 1941. Christmas. For dinner, they went to Murray's.

On the Monday, Matthew had a letter from Rupert.

I was rite, it told him. *She brot me to New York. It snoed and we had a Pullman. On Crismas I will miss you. We are going to have hour diner in the dining room downstairs. Theres a tree with angels on it and a star.*

Mother says we can wish for anything we want and one day it will all com true. She says thats life. Take care of you for me. Rupert.

At the top of the page, printed in burgundy letters, Matthew read:

THE WALDORF-ASTORIA
NEW YORK CITY

Still afloat.

20th January, 1942

At school, Matthew had continual encounters with his father's image. Also with the austere, immaculate image of Ian in his cricket whites. *Forbes Primus* and *Forbes Secondus*. Heroes of a different stamp. Not for Ian the muddied fields — nor for Graeme the academic trophies. All these events were shown in framed, glassed-over photographs: field days, prize days, football triumphs — from 1912, when Ian was a new boy, to 1922, on Graeme's graduation. Ten years of Forbes dominance, cut short by Ian's death and Graeme's departure — not for university, but for the world of stocks and bonds on Bay Street.

Matthew would stand before these treasures, hung as they were in corridors and the Common Room. There was his father, lightly padded in old-style football gear, his team the College Champions of 1921 or '22. Graeme seemed impossibly young, his feet in cleated boots, spread wide apart, and one arm hanging down, the other with the football cradled by his elbow — the centrepiece of all the world, his team rowed up around him. Where had he gone, this man of infinite possibilities? Matthew had never known him — only the running shadow in the park, whose stride had shortened and whose eye had glazed.

There, too, was Thomas Forbes, industrialist and member of the Board of Governors. And in the audience — this on the quad in June of 1916 — spread in dappled splendour, seated beneath the leafy arms of maple trees, all the parents of all the boys of glory. Matthew could see his grandmother, Ellen — Isabel beside her — each of them gowned exquisitely, each of them fixed on the blazered figure standing on the dais with his father — Ian receiving the Talbot Trophy for academic excellence from Tom's own hands. Doctor Macdonald, who was then Head Master, waited in his splendid gown to present Forbes Primus with the Marquis of Lorne Cup for Leadership. Weighted with his prizes, Ian would leave in two months' time for France — and not return.

"Is your father in any of these?" Matthew asked Rupert one evening in the Common Room.

"One," said Rupert, taking Matthew farther along the room and stopping before a photograph which showed the debating team of 1923. "There." Rupert laid a slender finger on a figure — pale and attenuated as himself, dressed in black or navy blue, its neck as long as any Matthew had ever seen, and its wrists, like Rupert's, boning out beyond its jacket cuffs. He seemed very tall, this man — this boy — and his gaze was blazing with fierce intelligence waiting to be articulated.

"What was his name?"

"Augustus Gilbert."

Augustus Gilbert Wright.

"He was a genius, my mother said."

Matthew blinked.

"She says he burned in the dark like a lamp, and all the moths would come and cluster around his mind."

They watched Augustus Gilbert for a moment then in silence — after which Matthew said: "what happened? You said he was dead."

"Oh, yes. When I was a child."

"You're still a child."

"But younger. Much. I was four."

"And so ...?"

"He went up a mountain and didn't come down."

Matthew said nothing. In his mind, he heard the wind. He saw the snow. He closed his eyes.

"Do you remember him?"

"Sort of. What I remember is him teaching me how to read. But I forgot it all when he died. Also, I remember ..."

"What?"

"The smell of the books we read. And his fingernails laid along the words."

Finally, Rupert gave his father one last look and turned away. "I never say it's him," he said. "I heard McAlpine saying once he thought it was the ugliest face he'd ever seen — next to mine."

"McAlpine is an ass," said Matthew.

"Yes. But everyone likes him."

This was true.

In the night, the boys and men in these photographs would haunt the darkened dormitory — gathered in their silent magnificence, cleated, gowned and windblown — muddied, whited, lost. Snow blew over them all and Matthew slept in the drifting of it. His father came and stood above him — seventeen years old. The football rested still in the crook of his arm, and then he put it down by Matthew's side, gave it one last touch and turned away.

Dad?

Nothing.

The wind had taken him back into the blizzard, out to the foot of the mountain where he stopped and, gazing upward, waited for the mountain-top to come to him.

21st January, 1942

The Officers' Mess at Trenton was a wide, long room, furnished in pale blond wood and summery chintz. Tables, overloaded with magazines and lamps, stood behind the sofas and beside the chairs. There were so many lamps, in fact — with such a variety of shades — that it seemed the Requisitions Officer had thought he was meant to light an entire hotel.

There were windows along two walls, and doors to the south that led to a terrace. Drapes were drawn at night. This gave the room a clubbish atmosphere, suggesting the world could be held at bay with a bit of cloth. French doors, rarely closed, led to and from an anteroom and a corridor leading to various administration offices and quarters. The floor was covered with bare, heavy-duty red linoleum — highly polished. Many leather heels had long ago made their mark, which gave a pebbled effect. Portraits of various Air Marshals — Billy Bishop chief amongst them — and of other aeronautic heroes were hung on the walls. The C.O. had thoughtfully made sure there was a piano and, on occasion, a dance band was brought in on weekends. Wives and *sweethearts* — a word Graeme loathed — were invited to soirées once a month in winter and every week in the summer. Drinks were bought with chits and the barman, a civilian, wore a short white jacket. It all reminded Graeme of an ocean-liner lounge — barring the absence of ground swell.

His first encounters with the mess were somewhat intimidating. *What do they know about me? What have they heard?* But Roy stood by him and, though he drank, he never drank to excess. Roy had said: *the only thing I ask is that we don't become an item.*

This had made Graeme laugh, an event so rare that even he had begun to wonder what his teeth looked like. *Good morning, Mister Grim-guts,* he would say to his image in the bathroom mirror, *got any dimples for me today? How about a Shirley Temple?*

His room-mate didn't help. McColl was so damned athletic and so damned young. He practically tap-danced his way out of bed every morning. Walked around naked, showing off his muscles. He'd laid half the female population of Trenton, to hear him tell it. *No wife — no kids — just dames.*

"Don't go on about it, Gray. It's boring," said Roy. "The young are always with us. He's not a bad kid, in fact. He speaks very well of you."

"Does he?"

"Sure he does. Why not?"

"I assumed he thought I was an asshole, being in the doldrums all this time. An older man — not a pilot and all. Not much to offer a twenty-year-old. And sure as hell not much fun."

"Forget it."

Now, McColl was leaving — posted to Halifax.

"My old stomping grounds," Graeme told Roy. "I had a bad time there. Mi came — you remember? There was a woman name of Tatiana Grosvenor. Do you believe it? Tatiana Grosvenor!"

"Yes, I remember. You've told me about her."

"Yes?"

"Many times." Roy sighed. "Come on, Gray — lighten up. It's all in the past."

That had been a week ago. Now, there was to be a farewell party for McColl in the mess. For McColl and eleven others who had been posted to Halifax with him. Mostly pilots on their way to Coastal Command.

"The U-boats are getting so cocky, they surface in Halifax harbour!" someone had joked. "The crews slip into town, get drunk in the bars, screw all the local women and depart at dawn. Happens all the time."

"Yeah. There's kids being born with Hitler's moustache."

The party had started at eight.

At nine, the C.O. had left the mess, having wished them all well, in the hopes they would enjoy themselves for the rest of the evening.

They did.

It began with a steeplechase, followed by a game of touch football. Graeme could not resist.

He made an end run around the piano and was cheered. He threw a forward pass to Roy that avoided all the lamps and gave them another touchdown. Then he ran the entire field without being tagged and won the game.

"Whew!" said Roy. "I didn't know you still had it in you, kid. That was terrific!"

"Yeah?"

"Yeah!"

"Yeah?"

"*Yeah!*"

Many slaps on the back. Some cuffing on the chin. A cheer. And someone calling him *Forbsey*.

It was school again. Hero time.

By eleven, he was playing the piano. McColl and others brought him drinks. He played "Barney Google" — he played "The Whiffenpoof Song" — he played "The Camptown Races,"

"Swanee River" and "Waltzing Matilda." Then he played "Tipperary, Bless 'Em All" and "I've Got Sixpence." Everybody sang.

> *I've got sixpence,*
> *Jolly, jolly sixpence.*
> *I've got sixpence,*
> *To last me all my life!*
> *I've got tuppence to spend!*
> *And tuppence to lend!*
> *And tuppence to send home to my wife!*
> *Poor wife.*

There was then a lot of cheering and a horse race in which the losing side in the football game had to play mounts to the departing pilots. McColl won.

Graeme gave him a push.

It was meant to be a friendly shove, but — just as his arm went out, for no reason at all, he saw red.

"You son of a bitch!" he said.

He didn't mean it. He just said it.

"Hey — hey! No swearing in the mess."

Roy said — quietly taking Graeme aside to say it: "enough. You've had enough."

"Never had enough. Not ever."

"Come on, Gray."

"I'VE NEVER HAD FUCKING ENOUGH! NEVER! ALL YOU BASTARDS ARE ALWAYS TRYING TO STOP ME!"

Roy held his arm — but lightly.

"Let go," said Graeme — now barely audible.

"It's time to stop, Gray. Time to go to bed."

"No — no." Graeme smiled, but it was ugly. A death's head smile. "Nooo-nooo. Never bedtime. One more drink — then, I promise."

Roy waited until he felt the energy draining from Graeme's arm. Then he said: "okay. *One*." And let go.

Graeme was calm — but wavering. He took a step forward and sat down in the nearest chair. "I'll have it here," he said.

Roy went over to the bar, telling the barman that he would take care of Flying Officer Forbes. Then he ordered a watered Scotch for Graeme and a double for himself.

A very few men who had lingered in Graeme's vicinity drifted back to the party — where the last wild act of the night was taking place. A pilot named Gregson was going around with a pair of scissors and ceremoniously cutting off the ties of the departing others. He then cut off his own tie and waved all the remnants in the air above his head like a victorious matador.

"For King and Country!" he shouted. And all the others shouted after him. "King and Country! Do or Die!"

This was followed by one last cheer. And then another pianist took Graeme's place at the piano.

Roy came back with their drinks.

"There you go."

"Than's."

There was only one song left to sing on such a night.

> *Should old acquaintance be forgot*
> *And never brought to mind;*
> *Should old acquaintance be forgot,*
> *And the days of auld lang syne.*

Graeme gave a cry and tipped his drink into his lap.

"Oh, God," he said to Roy, "take me home."

Roy got him up. No one heard them. No one saw them depart. The song went on.

By the door, a Junior Officer stepped forward. Roy had never seen him before.

"Can I help?"

"No thanks," said Roy. "I ..."

"No. Please," the young man said.

Graeme could barely see him.

"I'm Henderson."

"Henderson?" This was Roy.

"Yes, sir. I'm going to be Flying Officer Forbes's new room-mate." He was smiling, but kindly. He took Graeme's elbow and said to Roy: "I guess I should get used to this." And then: "don't worry. I've had lots of practice."

Roy did not ask for an explanation. But he liked the look of Henderson, who reminded him of the photographs he'd seen of Spitfire pilots and racing drivers. Cool. Sure. Knowing.

"We go in here," Roy said.

"I'll turn on the lights."

"No, don't. He wouldn't like it. Let's put him to bed like this."

They removed Graeme's shoes and took off his jacket and tie, drew down his braces and opened the top of his fly — while Graeme sat nodding in the spill of light from the hall. Then they helped him lie down and covered him with a blanket.

"Good night."

There was no reply.

As they started through the doorway, Graeme spoke — but only Roy heard him.

"Am I home yet?"

"Yes. Good night."

Turning back to the doorway, Roy found Henderson gone. He smiled. *That*, he thought, *is what I call tact*.

14th February, 1942

Valentine's Day fell on a Saturday and Graeme was able to get the weekend. Mi took the train to Trenton and booked a room at The Green Parrot. Graeme had to work until mid-afternoon, so Mi went shopping and came back to the hotel with beer and Scotch, flowers and six tins of sardines, a box of soda crackers, a flat-fifty of cigarettes and a jar of Planter's Peanuts.

Splurge. Why not.

The Green Parrot was relatively famous. All the wives stayed there whenever their husbands got a pass and it had a pleasant dining-room and comfortable beds. It had once been somebody's house — almost a mansion — with tall brick chimneys, curving roofs and wide, vaguely tropical verandahs where people sat in wicker chairs or left their galoshes by the door, depending on the season. There were trees and lawns and a Green Parrot sign that practically talked, the painted bird was so real. Also, a tower, whose windows were curved and hung with ferns. It was charming.

When Graeme arrived, all Mi could think was how small he looked in his greatcoat. Small and thin. Not well.

She met him in the hall, having watched his arrival from the sitting-room. Just after lunch, the floors had been waxed and polished. The smells of lemon oil and kerosene were rampant.

"Never mind, Gray," said Mi. "We can close the door. And I've got some lovely flowers."

Graeme gave a nod, having not yet spoken. He held his hat in one hand and his overnight bag in the other.

In the bedroom, Mi took his coat and hung it in the closet. Graeme set his bag on the bed and opened it.

"They're expecting Singapore to fall," he said — as if she had come all this way to hear the war news. His back was to her.

"Oh?" In the closet, the hangers jangled along the rail — a sound Mi hated.

"Today — tomorrow — any minute. Same old story. Can't defend themselves. Idiot guns. Remember the Maginot Line in France? Only fired in one direction. In Singapore, the guns fire out to sea. And of course — the Japs came down behind them. Overland on bicycles, for God's sake. A bunch of Japs on bikes — and we lose it all. Hopeless." Graeme sat on the bed — with his shaving kit in his lap.

Mi said: "it's not as if Singapore was around the corner, Gray. We're safe." She laughed.

"Sure. Safe. But we're going to lose the war."

"Don't say that. I won't hear it. Not another word about losing." She looked at him. His eyes were closed. "Can't we talk about something else?"

"That's all there is."

"There's me," she said. "You could tell me how I look."

"You look fine."

"Oh? How can you tell?"

Graeme opened his eyes.

"There! See? My new hair-do? All pinned up. It's the latest thing. No more curlers — no more permanent waves! Brush it out — pile it on top! I love it. Quick and comfortable. Cheap. And I look — well — maybe just a little like Rita Hayworth."

She posed.

"Very nice."

"Also — I have sardines. I have soda crackers. I have beer. Just like all the old times — all our old Saturdays, Gray. Remember? We'd ditch the kids and have the whole world to ourselves in that nutty cottage up at Shanty Bay?"

"Sure."

"And — ta-*da!* — I brought you this."

An envelope.

Graeme stared.

"Open it. No beer and sardines till you do."

"What is it?"

"*Open it,* you goof!"

Graeme took the envelope and peeled it apart.

"Oh, God," he said.

"What's the matter?"

"It's today. Valentine's."

"Yes. It's today."

Graeme spread his hand flat out across his eyes and lowered his head.

Mi was alarmed. She went and sat beside him.

"Don't," she said. "It's all right. It's all right. Don't. Please don't. It doesn't matter. Everyone forgets."

She put her arm around his shoulder. He wept.

Mi looked out the window, past the flowers in their pressed-glass vase and the photograph of Matthew and Bonnie, silver-framed and her constant companion.

A long, long time ago I met this man at a party. A long, long time ago — and ... she took Graeme's hand *... he was playing the piano. I took one look — I took one look and said:* don't anybody tell me who that is. He's dangerous. I'm in danger ...

She looked down.

93

Those long, slim fingers. That long, slim body. That long, slim grin ...
She smiled and pulled him closer.

I went across that room — wherever it was — somebody's private ball-room — 1926 — and I stood behind these broad, boy shoulders and I watched while he played. Played — and hoisted a glass — and played again. And I sat down ... sat down and said: what's that you're playing? And who are you ..."

Oh, God. Who are you now? Who are you now?

"Don't cry," she said. "Don't."

Graeme extricated himself and, taking his shaving kit, went into the bathroom.

Mi sat — desolate. *We've lost,* she thought. *We've lost the war to save each other.*

"Graeme?"

He came and stood in the bathroom door. He had a wad of toilet paper in his hand and blew his nose into it.

"You want to go to bed?" said Mi.

Graeme blinked. His eyes were still wet.

"Sure," he said. "But later." He turned away. "Why don't you crack a couple of beer and open those sardines?"

The door closed.

Mi waited.

Sure. But later.

She heard the taps — first one and then the other, sputter and spout.

She stood up.

The sardines, soda crackers and peanuts were in the bureau. The beer was in the closet. *It won't be cold, of course. I should have thought to ask for ice.*

"Graeme?"

94

Taps.

"I'm going downstairs to get some ice. Okay?"

Splashing.

Mi pushed the Johnny Walker Red Label out of the way and brought down the beer — two quart bottles. Then she hid the rest in her suitcase. For later — after.

Mi went into the hall and down the stairs. The image of the Scotch and beer bottles lingered in her mind. Bringing the liquor had been her own idea. She'd thought about it all the way down on the train. *If we drink together, he'll know that I trust him. See that I trust him. Think that I do — and then he won't go off the rails.*

She paused on the landing.

Down below her, near the reception desk, were two other couples.

Air Force. Young. Signing in. A dashing blond with a clinging brunette and a dashing brunet with a clinging blonde. There was snow on their hats and in their hair and sprinkled over their shoulders. *They look like Christmas decorations — paper-doll airmen — paper-doll dames — John Payne and Betty Grable — Alan Ladd and Paulette Goddard. Sort of.*

Mi started down again.

She could smell the women. Expensive perfume, but too much of it. The scent of it mingled with the lingering scent of floor wax and produced an oddly exotic flavour that Mi could taste with her tongue.

When she got to the desk, the paper-doll blonde was standing on tip-toe, picking snowflakes off her young man's shoulder. With her finger end, she put each one of them into her mouth.

"I just love snow!" she said. "Back home, I eat it all the time." Then she saw Mi and sank to her normal, high-heeled height — about five-foot-two.

With eyes of blue, Mi thought.

"Hello," said the girl, clinging tighter to Mister Beau's blue arm. Mi saw on his sleeve the giveaway insert on his forage cap. It was white.

Still in training. Maybe a pilot. Handsome. Almost pretty. Innocent, isn't-life-a-gas eyes — pale as sea-blue ice and barely a trace of human intelligence. A bouncing baby boy … baboon.

> *Now, stop that.*

> With a starlet on his arm. Two bits, she wears those shoes to bed.

> *You sound like Eloise.*

> I'm learning. I'm learning.

"Hello," Mi said — and turned away to the woman behind the desk. "Excuse me for interrupting, but we'd like some ice. Should I go to the kitchen, or what?"

"We'll have it sent up, Mrs Forbes. Just give me ten minutes to deal with these new arrivals."

"Thank you."

As Mi left, she distinctly heard Miss Snow-Eating Queen of 1942 say: "goodbye."

Mi turned.

After all, at least it's thoughtful of the child.

"Goodbye," she said — and smiled. "I hope you have a lovely weekend."

"Thanks. We're going to. It's our honeymoon." Plus a big, red smile.

Four hours later, Mi woke up to find herself alone in the bed. The room smelled of beer and sardines.

Good Lord! It's after seven!

"Gray?"

He was in the bathroom. Showering.

Mi pushed the covers back and stood up.

Looking at herself in the mirror, she winced at what had become of her hair. By lamplight, she looked like her mother. Old.

She lighted a cigarette.

In the bathroom, the showering continued.

Why couldn't he sing, like everyone else? Of course, he'll feel terrible. We've never had this happen before.

Mi went over to the bathroom door and looked in. What she saw was mostly steam.

"We're booked for dinner at eight."

Nothing.

"Gray?"

He did not reply.

"Darling?"

Mi went in and spoke to the shower curtain.

"You're making an awful lot of steam, my dear one. Don't you think that's enough?"

What the hell's going on?

"At least you could answer."

When this produced nothing, Mi pulled the curtain.

There was no one there. Just running water — and roiling steam.

He was gone. So was the Johnny Walker Red Label.

He hadn't found the rest of the beer.

At eight o'clock, Mi went down to the dining-room and ate her dinner alone. Lamb chops, mashed potatoes and dyed green peas from a can. Her food was afloat in a pale green flood.

Two cigarettes — with her eye on the door, John Payne and Betty Grable, Alan Ladd and Paulette Goddard obscuring her view. Laughing.

Unwanted apple pie à la mode. Coffee. Two more cigarettes and back to the room.

"Good night," as she passed.

This time, no reply.

All night long, Mi waited — awake. She drank the beer and fell asleep at dawn. Her last thought was: impotence doesn't last forever. Surely he knows that. I know it — so must he.

Men don't talk about it.

Maybe not. But they should. Oh, dear — now what ...?

After that, it was noon — and after that, time for Mi to go. Her train left at four.

Trying to phone Graeme, but all she had been told was: *I'm sorry, Mrs Forbes, he can't talk to you now* — and no explanation.

As if you needed one.

The train left on time. *And wouldn't it just?*

There was snow. A blizzard.

As Mi went home, at seven-thirty eastern standard time that evening, nine thousand miles away on the other side of the world, the British Garrison at Singapore fell.

There is a photograph of Mi and Ellen. Also one of Isabel and Mi. They are seated on the back porch steps at Foxbar Road, wearing overcoats. Pale spring sunlight whitens their faces, almost erasing lines and features. Three women alone together, each in her separate world, each world's borders meeting in the hinterland. Silence between them.

Ellen's eyes are closed. I am not here. *Mi's cast their glance at her feet.* Whose feet are these? *Only Isabel stares at the camera.* Don't look at me like that. It isn't seemly.

Where has everyone gone?

There will be tea and sherry, later. Mi will drink Scotch in her room and so long as Ellen remains downstairs, she will also be able to play her gramophone. Ellen does not care for music. She favours radio comedies: Fibber McGee and Molly. Charlie McCarthy. Fanny Brice. Jack Benny. *The laughter from Ellen's radio floats up past the landing and along the hall. The music does not float down. Rachmaninoff.*

Mi thinks: I am France. I have surrendered.

Then she thinks: I can't do that. I can't just let it end. That's what my mother did: laid down her arms. Pulled down her flag. She sank to her knees and died.

I won't do that. I won't.

Then there is a photograph of Mi with flowers at Bonnie's grave. May 25, 1942. Bonnie's eighth birthday. If. Mi turns and tries to smile at Eloise, who takes the picture. See? But the smile does not materialize.

A letter arrives from Trenton, Ontario.

Mi reads it in the kitchen.

Ellen watches and says: what's wrong?

Mi says: nothing.

She goes to the living-room and sets the letter on fire — watches it flame and drops it like a falling aeroplane into the grate.

Looking up from what she has done, she catches Ian watching her from the mantel. Lucky you, *she says.* You'll never know.

When she goes upstairs, she slams her door.

1st June, 1942

It was Friday, the first in the month and the day before the Bests' anniversary. Eloise had come to Trenton to celebrate with Roy and to scout out likely boarding houses for Mi. Because Mi was nervous of broaching the subject of her summer plans with Graeme, it had been decided that quarters had to be secured before she told him.

"*Fait accompli*, that's what we need. A *fait accompli*, so he can't say nay."

Eloise had thought Mi was crazy and said so: "you're only going to make things worse when he finds out you've been sneaking around behind his back."

"*Me* sneaking around behind *his* back! You've got to be joking."

"Why not just say: *I'm thinking of coming, and …*"

"What's wrong with: *here I am, and here I'll stay?* Dammit."

"Why throw down the gauntlet? There isn't any evidence he's playing around."

"Ho."

"Ho, yourself. There isn't."

Mi was silent.

"Is there?"

Mi looked away.

"Michael. Answer me."

"Her name is Sue Anne Howard."

"Jesus. You know her name. Sue Anne Howard?"

"So I'm told."

"Oh. I see. The grapevine again. Officers' wives ought to learn to mind their own damn business."

"I'm an officer's wife."

"Yes — and so am I. But I don't dish the dirt on other girls' husbands. Sue Anne Howard is probably just some dame who made goo-goo eyes at the wrong man and the wrong man's wife is getting even by telling everyone she's a tramp. You should know better than to pay attention to crap like that. Who is she, anyway — Sue Anne Howard?"

"I don't know."

"There you go, then. Who the hell told you all this?"

"Someone anonymous."

"Oh, for Pete's sake, Mi! For Pete's bloody sake! *Someone anonymous?* I don't believe it. How did she sign herself? *Your loyal friend?*"

"Yes, as a matter of fact."

"Where is this idiot letter? Let me see it."

"I burned it."

"Oh — terrific! You burned it. Oh, *please!*"

"Stop that. *Stop that.* Stop making fun of me. It's serious."

"Sorry. Of course it is." And then: "women are strangely cruel, Mi. You may not have noticed. Cruel, I mean, to one another. Not that men aren't cruel — but when men are cruel, they kill.

They get it over with. Women prefer a lingering death. Men accuse. Women insinuate. Men knock you down. Women string you up. I don't know which is worse."

Eloise had walked away from Mi at this point. They had been standing in Ellen's living-room. It was the first of June. In the garden, out beyond the open windows, birds were singing. Robins. An oriole.

"I can remember," Eloise went on, "when I had my first period — and how mysterious it was — to bleed without being wounded. Hurt. No falling down — no knives — just blood. I wasn't frightened. I wasn't in pain — I was just amazed. I had a friend who'd started before me. We'd discussed it — but we were ignorant. So, when I went to my mother and said: *what does it mean?* — she said: *it means that you're a woman. You will suffer this all your life.* Not *welcome to the wonders of womanhood* — but *Oh, you poor child* — *the cost! The price! The disaster that awaits you!* Then, of course, she spent the next week describing *the horrors of penetration* and *the terrors of childbirth!* You see what I mean? It's not all women, but it's *only* women who do that to each other. They want revenge for having to suffer the *indignity* — hoo-ha! — of being female. We're all so *vulnerable*. We can't *fight back*. It isn't *ladylike* to brawl. So what they do is pull you down into their own hurt. Don't you see? *You deserve it.* That's what they want you to believe. It's your due. If they can prove your husband is unfaithful, you're only getting what's coming to you. *It's nature's way of dealing with the daughters of Eve.* After all, you're only a woman — only *another* woman, like *poor li'l me.* Boo-hoo."

Mi could not help smiling. Eloise always got so wound up in what she was saying — playing all the parts — using all her voices — waving her arms — blowing smoke and gulping air.

Out on the lawn, the robins were searching for worms and a squirrel was chattering at them from a tree.

"I've had letters like that," said Eloise. "From *loyal friends* — *anonymous* donors to the world's misery. Every wife has. All about *your husband and that well-known slut, Miss So-and-so.* Writing snitch-notes — it's a profession. *Whoopee! I've just destroyed someone else's happiness. Bully for me!*"

That night, Eloise took Mi to see *Woman of the Year*, with Katharine Hepburn and Spencer Tracy. When they came out, Mi said: "it was perfect until the end. Then she had to go and marry him."

Eloise thought: *okay. You can't win.*

Now, a week later, Eloise was sitting in The Green Parrot, dining with Roy.

"You ever meet a lady called Sue Anne Howard?" she asked.

Roy looked away. "Sure," he said.

Eloise felt her stomach knot. She set down her fork. Roy looked back at her.

"Nice kid," he said.

"Kid?"

"Yeah. Twenty-one — twenty-two."

"Local?"

"I don't know where she's from. Hamilton. Could be. He was born in Hamilton."

"He?"

"Yeah. Billy Howard."

Roy ate. Eloise watched him.

"Air Force?"

"Unh-hunh."

"Would you call her a sweet young thing — this Sue Anne Howard — or a slut?"

Roy nearly choked. When he recovered, he looked at Eloise as if she had just drawn a gun.

"What the hell kind of question is that?"

Eloise flushed. She had not really known she was going to be quite so precise.

"A childish question," she said. "And I apologize."

"And so you should. My God ..." Roy shook his head. "You really take the cake."

"I said I was sorry." Eloise looked at her uneaten food. "How long have you known her?"

"I dunno. A month. Two months. Three. What difference does it make?"

"Is she having an affair with Graeme Forbes?"

"Jesus Christ, Eloise. Where is all this coming from?"

Eloise was still looking at her plate. She felt nauseated and had to swallow twice before she was able to speak again.

"Is she fucking Graeme Forbes?"

Roy pushed his chair back and almost stood up.

"You're in uniform," said Eloise. "Don't make a scene."

They sat for a moment in absolute silence. Then Roy said: "I'm not Gray's keeper, but I'll tell you this much — I'm not going to talk about him behind his back."

Eloise bit her lip. Her eyes filled with tears. She raised her head and looked away to one side. "You don't know what it feels like," she said, "to be a woman in this bloody situation. You men — you men all have each other. And we're all apart!" Her voice rose. "You don't know what it feels like!"

"May I remind you that you are with a man in uniform. Don't make a scene."

"I'm not making a scene!"

The couple at the next table had turned to watch and listen.

Eloise glared at them and said: "leave us alone."

The couple called for their bill.

"Good riddance," said Eloise under her breath. Then she blew her nose. When she was more or less composed, she looked at Roy as best she could and said: "listen to me. Listen. It's the distance that does it. The *distance*. And always being alone with other women — most of them troubled — all of them single. Even married, they're all single. *I'm* single. Do you understand that? I'm an unmarried, married woman. And what I have every day is Mother ..." She gave a wry laugh. "I'm sure you can appreciate what a blast that is. *Ellie do* — and *Ellie don't!* But at least someone's paying attention. Even if it's not my gorgeous husband. But — Mi has nothing. No one. Bonnie dead. Mattie at school. Ellen and Isabel like fish. And all this bloody distance. Jesus Christ! Stop staring at me as if I was mad. I love you. I love you. And look where you are! All the way over there on the other side of the table!"

Roy stood up.

"Sit down. It's still my turn."

Roy sat — almost like a child — with his hands in his lap.

"It's normal," Eloise said. "It's perfectly normal to be afraid. To be afraid you're going to lose your husband. He looks so damned good in his uniform — even Bela Lugosi would look like Gary Cooper, in a uniform. But you're only wearing the god-damned uniform because of the *fucking war* ..."

"Don't."

"Stop! I'm all right. Leave me alone. I want to finish. This fucking war — and you in that uniform — if you don't know what it means, I *do: someone's gonna getcha, Roy. Roy, baby!* Some gun — some girl is gonna getcha — who cares which? It's all death. That's what's happening to us. To all of us. We're being killed. Killed by distance. By silence. Everyone out of sight — out of earshot — out of touch. Everyone — unreachable."

Roy was silent.

"There," said Eloise, and sat back. "Done."

After a moment, Roy said: "you want to go upstairs to bed?"

"Yes."

"Two whole nights and two whole days."

"Yes."

And then: "you're still not certain, are you."

"About you — yes. Not about Gray. And I just can't bear the thought of what's going to happen to Mi."

"All I can tell you ..."

"Yes? What?" Her stomach began to knot again.

Roy was trying to be matter-of-fact. He spoke as if reporting to a senior officer.

"Billy Howard was killed here six weeks ago. In a training acci-dent. He crashed. Sue Anne Howard is his widow. And ..." He took a deep breath and exhaled. "Graeme takes her mind off things. She's really just a big-eyed kid. A child who got hurt — in a grown-up situation. Billy was the same. I was his instructor. Just a big, enthusiastic child with a toy. Not too bright, but gutsy. Two kids — playing some kind of game. He played the man — she played the woman ..."

"*Married people.*"

"That's right. *Playing house.*"

Eloise sniffed.

"Graeme sure is some kind of bastard."

"Yes. I hate to admit it — but I guess he is."

Eloise shook her head. "Billy Howard. Learning how to fly."

"Yep."

"Why do all the wrong people die? Answer: *so all the others can get to sleep with their wives.*"

"You don't believe that, hon."

"No. I don't. I just wish I could be that cold-blooded."

"Lucky for me, you can't."

10th July, 1942

Mi and Matthew went down to Trenton on a Friday. The train was so crowded, many had to stand — some in the aisles, others on the platforms between the cars. The heat was palpable, blinding them with sweat and clinging like a second skin to the undersides of clothes. It was so oppressive that, in spite of soot and cinders, all the windows had been opened.

Boarding in the first wave of passengers, Mi and Matthew had managed to find two inside seats, sitting opposite one another with Mi's Victrola and record case beneath their feet on the floor between them. On Mi's left side, a tall silent woman sat with a cardboard cake box in her lap and an open Bible held up close to her face. Her companion must have been a grandchild, the woman being in her late fifties. Matthew was able to watch this child, a girl, and was fascinated by the fact that she didn't speak once, the entire journey. She wore a pale blue dress, white socks and white shoes. Also, white gloves. Six, Matthew guessed — or seven, at the most.

He looked at Mi. She was staring out the window, already *there* — at Trenton with his father.

Beyond the windows, the sun was shining and the sky was blinding. High, wide and blue — the blue so hot it was almost white. *Clickety-click — clackety-clack,* he drummed with his fingers on the sill.

Brahms, Mi was thinking. *Did I bring the Brahms?* She tried to make up an image of all the music clustered beneath her feet. The Rachmaninoff *Paganini Variations,* the Gershwin *Piano Concerto,* the

Brahms *Third Symphony* ... what else? "These Foolish Things," "Smoke Gets in Your Eyes," "My Bonnie," "You'll Never Know" ... The story of our lives, Gray. The story of our lives.

Clickety-click — to Halifax. *Clackety-clack* — to Trenton. She felt like Ruth, in the Bible. Graeme was her Naomi: *whither thou goest, I will go*. Damn right. And dammit.

In the baggage car, there were two suitcases, a cardboard box and a steamer trunk, all with *M.M. FORBES* in black stencilled letters. First, she was Michael Maude Fulton. Now, she was Michael Maude Forbes. She smiled, remembering.

Michael Maude! Michael Maude! her mother used to call. *Michael Maude! Michael Maude!* At dusk, from an upstairs window. *Michael Maude, you come in, now — darkness is falling.* Darkness always fell, light always rose.

Mi looked across and smiled at Matthew, wondering how — when he was her age and she was gone into the past — he would remember her. Whenever she called him in from the dark, she tried to avoid her mother's singsong cadences — no *Matthew Tom* for him! He would have killed her. *Mattie! Get in here!* That's what she called. And then: *this instant!* She prided herself that she could stand at the bottom of the garden, top of the hill, and hit the other side of the ravine with her voice. Almost all the way to Whitewood's Stables.

Not so loud! You'll scare the horses!

Named for his father and grandfather, Matthew wasn't like either of them. Not remotely. Self-possessed and distant. Mi always thought of him as living in a body one size smaller than his being — part of him always rushing forward beyond the rest of him, leaving part of him behind. *A skin-tight boy, my darling — that's what you are, sitting over there across from me. Skin-tight, expressionless — and your self made up of dreams and stories — Boy Carton — Boy Balfour — Boy Hannay. I know all your heroes, my dear one — I gave you the books in which you found them.*

She looked away.

I'm doing it again. Damn me. Dragging him away from safety — carting him off like a package.

She looked at him. He wasn't watching.

Clickety-click.

I'll say this for him: he drags with dignity.

So many servicemen got off the train at Trenton, Mi was afraid that Matthew would be swept away — carried off in the khaki tide of summer. "Follow me," she said, "and don't take your eyes off my back for one second."

They went along the platform to the station itself, where a knot of other women and children had already formed. Mi had no expectations Graeme would meet them. Still, it would be nice if he was there. Or someone. A staff car and a driver. *Flying Officer Forbes has sent me, ma'am. I'm here to take you to your destination. Let me carry that for you ...* and all the luggage whisked away and put in the back of a station wagon.

Wouldn't that be the day!

The knot of civilians grew in size. Ten. A dozen. Fifteen. They greeted one another with cordial shyness — all attempting to endure the same confusion as if they knew precisely what would happen next. Mi thought there wasn't a single concern reflected on the women's faces she didn't recognize as being her own. And every child, no matter what age, had an expression shared with animals put in cages: *where are we going — and what will be done with us?*

The only porters were slow old men trying to get all the luggage onto a single baggage cart. Under any other circumstances, Mi would have gone and collected her own suitcases, but she knew the old men would resent this and, besides, she didn't dare leave Matthew. His habit of wandering off could be disastrous, if ...

"Mrs Forbes?"

Mi turned.

A man.

Mi had to shade her eyes from the sun in order to see him.

"Yes?"

He was in uniform — an officer — and he was smiling.

"I'm Gray's room-mate, Ivan Henderson," he said.

So this is the legendary Henderson ... Ivan.

"I recognize you from your picture on Gray's bureau."

"Oh, yes."

"Uhm ..." He looked around. "I've brought a car. It's not a Rolls Royce, I'm afraid. Just a station wagon, but it was all I could grab. Is there much? I mean luggage."

Mi had been watching him, amused — even delighted. Henderson was all charm and busy words — hat on — hat off and "this is Matthew?" and "let me get that for you" — lifting the Victrola — hoisting the record box and looking around for the rest — but never once not smiling.

The other women seemed to be equally captivated. And envious. While Henderson dealt with the steamer trunk, the box and the suitcases, Mi just stood there, beaming. *Mine.* It wasn't everyone, after all, who got to be greeted, assisted and driven away by Tyrone Power.

"I just can't thank you enough," said Mi. "You've saved our lives."

"Not to worry," said Ivan. "Truth to tell, I was glad to have an excuse to get off the base. It's like an oven there."

"So was the train," said Mi, "but this is heaven."

She was sitting up in the passenger seat while Ivan drove. Matthew, ensconced in a fortress of luggage, was riding in the back. The windows had all been rolled down and the draught had caught his hair in a whirlwind above his head.

"I smell water," he said.

"Lake Ontario," Ivan explained. "You'll see it in a moment. Bay of Quinte."

They had driven out of town across a high-piered bridge above the Trent River and now, turning south, they were passing through a shady, wooded area.

"All this was farmland before the Air Force came," Ivan told them. "Too bad we've ruined it, but I guess it was irresistible. Flat as a table top." Coming out of the wood, he gestured and said: "behold — the Bay of Quinte!"

"Very pretty," said Mi.

"Pretty, hell — it's beautiful!"

Mi laughed.

"I sail out there, sometimes."

"I haven't been sailing for years," Mi said. "I love it."

Matthew had never sailed.

"Here comes the base," said Ivan. "Be prepared for the longest chain-link fence in the world."

"Is it really?" said Mi.

"Well — no. I don't know — but it certainly seems it."

They began to pass along an avenue — almost a high wire tunnel — of fencing. *The kind they use in prison movies,* Matthew thought; *with Humphrey Bogart and James Cagney climbing over —*

*falling down the other side — while guards with searchlights and tommy-
guns pick them off, rat-a-tat ...*

"You should look the other way," Henderson told him. "That's
where the planes are."

Now, Matthew saw for the very first time the wide expanse of
landing fields — a prairie with seeming miles and miles of criss-
crossed runways and rows of mysterious hangars.

All along the tarmac, lined up in series, were dozens of yellow
aeroplanes. Even from inside the moving station wagon, Matthew
could hear them running up their engines. It was the loudest noise
he had ever heard. Far from the whine he'd expected, it was more
like a torrent of sound in which a person could drown. He covered his ears. It was awful. Later, he would think the noise defined
what was happening to him — everything blown away, and the
roar of its departure leaving him transfixed.

"Quite a racket, eh?" said Ivan.

Matthew could not speak.

All at once, the aeroplanes gave way to more dark hangars and,
beyond the hangars, a staff car — racing along the runway,
ghosting their own forward movement.

"Why is everyone in such a hurry?" Mi asked.

Ivan laughed.

"You think that's fast?" he said. "Watch this."

Sitting back, he began to gun the motor.

Mi looked over at him. *He's a pilot, of course, so I guess he's going
to fly us home.* The road, she was glad to see, was straight as the
proverbial die — and not a single other vehicle all the way to the
horizon.

"Everybody okay?" Henderson asked.

Neither of them answered.

Mi was thinking of Eloise and her erratic driving. *Watch out! Slow down!* But this was not like that. This was different. Somehow, she felt entirely safe.

Matthew closed his eyes and held his breath.

When the speedometer hit eighty, Mi said: "what do you fly, Mister Henderson? Rockets?"

"Why not?" said Henderson, smiling at her sideways. "Me and Buck Rogers."

At last, he began to ease the pressure along his thigh and down to his foot.

"Nearly there," he said.

Seventy-five. Seventy. Sixty-five. Sixty.

"I love this stretch of road," he said. "Sometimes, in the evening, I bring my Harley out here and fly all the way to Belleville!"

"A motorcycle?"

"Yep. Second great love of my life."

Mi was hesitant — not sure why. "And the first great love?" she asked.

"Anything with wings," he said — and grinned at her again. "Except maybe mosquitoes."

Matthew opened his eyes. *Where are we, now?* he wondered. They might have travelled a thousand miles in the last few seconds.

He could smell his mother's perfume.

He could smell his own body.

He could smell the acrid scent of burning fuel — the air in his mind made visible with its fumes.

Somewhere in all of this his father was waiting, hidden and unmentioned. It was as though they had come to a foreign country where Graeme did not exist — had never been heard of. Was dead.

A mile farther east along the road that cut the Air Base in two — and not quite half that distance down the first side road they came to — there was a sign.

The Willows. This was where they would spend the summer — kindness of Eloise and her excursions on Mi's behalf. *I have found you heaven itself,* she had said — and had not done it justice.

Five hundred yards of driveway, shaded by willow trees, led to a board-and-batten Victorian farmhouse — white and ringed with porches. A pair of barns was set another hundred yards along the drive and beyond these, a view of Jersey cows in sloping fields. Beyond their split-rail fences, the fields gave way to the reeds and rushes of a wide, slow-moving river running into the bay.

From the shadows on the porch, a woman came out to greet them, banging an old screen door behind her. This was Mrs Mortson, smiling and tall — standing in the sunlight, thinner than anyone Matthew had ever seen.

A dozen chickens rushed towards her over the grass, thinking she must have come to feed them, but Mrs Mortson ignored them and stood there squinting at her guests — nodding at Ivan and speaking his name: *Mister Henderson* — just as if he wasn't in the Air Force at all. Her thick grey hair spilled from beneath a blue bandanna and her feet were encased in enormous, man-sized shoes — perhaps her husband's.

Mi stepped forward to introduce herself and Mrs Mortson held her apron up to wipe her face — her cheeks and forehead white with flour. When she said: *hello there — greetings, call me Agnes,* her voice was cracked like the old blue-labelled records of Blossom Seeley Mi kept at home.

"Henry, Mister Mortson, is just gone over to the barns to do the milking," she explained. "Otherwise, he'd be here to help you with that steamer trunk." The steamer trunk, which Ivan had nearly ruptured himself depositing, sat at the edge of the driveway, looking impossibly out of place. "I'll show you to your rooms."

She picked up one of the cases from the grass and everyone followed her, carrying what they could — in through the kitchen, along the hallway and up the stairs to the rooms where Mi and Matthew would be sleeping. As she passed the open doors along the way, Agnes Mortson nodded at them, reciting: *parlour — dining-room — bathroom* ... She also mentioned an outhouse, *case of 'mergencies*.

Other guest-rooms told of other residents, but Mrs Mortson did not pause to name them. Matthew's room was at the back of the house, two doors away from Mi's. It was more than he had expected, with a chair and bureau and a double bed *all my own*. Through the window, he could see a dog and a tall, lean man he assumed was Mister Mortson, driving twenty Jersey cows towards the milking shed. It was perfect. It was crazy. Suddenly, more than anything in all the world, Matthew wanted to be a farmer.

When it came time for Ivan to leave, Mi went out and stood with him in the dust beside the steamer trunk. Matthew, having already said *goodbye*, preferred to stay in the shade of the porch, sitting on the top step.

The cicadas were singing, but no birds. Perhaps it was too hot. There were, however, chickens mewing on the lawn, where they were looking for insects. In the house, Mrs Mortson was singing in a creaking, wavering soprano about *the everlasting arms* as she went about the business of setting the dining-room table for the evening meal. In the fenced-in yard, by the milking shed, the cattle stood with cudding patience waiting for Mister Mortson's soothing hands to stroke them. Listening, Matthew heard what he would come to call "The Milking Song." It had no tune and no real words — just *soo-soo, lully-soo-soo* — as Mister Mortson drew down the milk, its rhythmic splashing a counterpoint, deepening in tone as the pail was filled.

Peace flooded through him. All sense of apprehension faded in the air around him, as the smells of willow leaves and cut grass, peonies and roses mingled with the barnyard smells of cow-breath, manure and hay and the faintest trace of gasoline from Mister Mortson's Massey-Harris tractor. When Matthew threw back his head, he could also smell the river.

His mother and Ivan were still talking — more than likely about his father. While he sat with his chin on his knees and watched, Matthew could hear only the sound of their voices, one and then the other — mostly Ivan's.

Ivan Henderson was taller than Graeme. Taller and tighter inside his body. While his father moved with the splayed, open steps of a long-distance runner, Ivan got from where he was to somewhere else the way an animal moves through the woods — stepping from stillness to stillness without being seen. His hands were square and brown and his fingers endlessly busied themselves with the edges of his peaked cap — and sometimes spun it like a top. As he talked, he turned from side to side and when he settled, he laid his forearms out along the top of the steamer trunk, looking like a sprinter waiting to take off down the track.

Ivan Henderson — speed star.

Mi's back was to Matthew. She held her right hand open against her forehead, the sun descending, caught in the trees behind the man in uniform. For the briefest moment, it might have been his father standing there — but Ivan put on his cap and was himself again. He gave a casual salute and called out *goodbye* to Matthew and was gone into the station wagon.

As the engine turned over and the car rolled forward, Mi stepped aside to let it pass. When it started down the driveway, she backed towards the steps, waved, and watched it all the way to the gate and onto the road.

When Matthew saw her face, he thought: *he's told her something,* and wondered what it was.

"Let's unpack," said Mi, and climbed the steps. At the top, as Matthew rose beside her, she turned and looked back into the yard and along the drive.

"Isn't it beautiful," she said. "For a change, we've landed on our feet."

> *The Willows,*
> *Trenton, Ontario,*
> *10.7.42*
>
> *Dear Eloise,*
> *I'm writing this as much for my sake as yours — not just to bring you up to date, but to get some order into the jumble in my head.*
> *We arrived more or less intact. The train was hell. The Willows is heaven. Thanks for finding it and talking me out of thinking we should be in the town. Matt adores it*

*already and so do I. The Mortsons are angels in disguise —
both of them characters and both of them delights. Rooms
comfortable, food scrumptious, other guests a mystery.*

*The big news is that something hopeful seems to be on the
books for Gray. His room-mate — a charmer name of
Henderson — met us at the train and got us here, bag and
baggage, as if he'd been hired by the Air Force specifically
to see that Mrs Forbes and son were well taken care of. (Is
that a preposition? Who gives a damn — I'm too excited
and can barely think!)*

Here's what's up.

*Ivan Henderson (he's a Pilot Officer) told me that Gray
had been having a pretty bad time ever since I was here in
February and you were here in June. He didn't mention the
bitch Sue Anne, but I guess he felt I didn't want to hear
about that — and who knows, maybe he thinks I've never
heard of her. Anyway, the good news is that Gray has
stopped drinking.*

!!!!!

I'm not even going to bother saying for the time being.
*Who cares if it's only for the time being? The thing is, he's
quit.*

*Ivan — (I think of him as Ivan, I might as well call him
that) — Ivan says it's all because the C.O. gave a damn
about Gray and his troubles and instead of throwing him
back down the stairs — or into the clink or whatever the
Air Force normally does with drunks — he offered him a
job!*

Not only a job, my dear, but a promotion to go with it!

A promotion, Ellie! A promotion!

119

*If the ink runs here, guess why. For the first time in years,
I'm crying for joy. Isn't it glorious? Isn't it beyond belief?
Flight Lieutenant Graeme Forbes. And sober. That's my
boy.*

*The job? He'll be Adjutant to the C.O. — meaning a
lot of responsibility — meaning a down-to-earth, real appli-
cation of Gray's administrative skills (which happen to be
considerable!) and*, above all, *requiring a lot of poise and
charm. Poise and charm, my darling. Remember the days
of G., all poise and charm and danger that was good, not
bad? He's back — the man I met and married.*

Oh my God. I can't believe it, but apparently it's true.

*The C.O.'s last name is Barker — (don't know his
first). You may have met him and I can't wait.*

*According to Ivan's report — when Gray hit bottom
(about the time you were here in June) Barker met with the
rest of the command and they discussed what should be
done. Most of the types were all for sending Gray back to
Borden — or worse — until he smartened up. Apparently
one man even thought Gray should be drummed right out
of the Service. Not Barker.*

*I think he must be some kind of gift from God — because
this is what he did. After the court martial (almost a court
martial) he called Ivan in (as Graeme's room-mate, I guess)
— and told him that Gray would be staying on. I sense
that Ivan has been close to Gray and good to him, but that
Gray has really been a handful. This was all through that
time when I didn't hear from him once and I thought the
world had ended.*

Ivan said Barker's reasoning had gone like this: "if you

hit a man when he's down, he may never get back up. But if you expect something of him — and say so — and put it to him — and give him new responsibilities, he'll regain his self-respect and do a good job."

And that's what happened.

I gather the only reason I haven't heard from Gray is because he was shaky at first, coming off the sauce, and wanted to be sure he was really standing on his own two feet before he made any promises.

Has he been drinking?

Ivan says no — but I suspect, a little — and I think Ivan knows it, too. But definitely not a lot, and definitely never to the point of drunkenness.

I'm so proud of him, I could scream.

Of course, this doesn't even begin to address the problem of Miss Garter Belts — (I see Sue Anne Howard wearing cheap lingerie, don't you?) — and it doesn't begin to address the problem of where our marriage stands. But it does address the problem of taking one step forward. Done. And wonderful.

It will mean so much to Mattie. He hasn't had a peep from Graeme for months and, I'm afraid, has really begun to hate him. Maybe this can stem the tide. I hope so.

I was beginning to believe I'd made a mistake — giving up the house — dragging Mattie down here. But now, I'm hopeful and think I might have done the right thing after all.

Any chance you can visit soon? You can sleep with me, if Mrs Mortson doesn't have a free room.

Oh, Lordy! Hallelujah!

Well, goodbye, my darling. Give my regards to your dreadful mother. And don't forget, the next time you see me, I'll be the Adjutant's Wife — so you'd better behave, babe.

See you later.

Much love,

Michael

That night, after finishing her letter to Eloise, Mi lay back on her bed and watched a spider walk across the ceiling.

Me, she thought. *The whole world upside down — but here we are, still moving forward.*

Leaning sideways, she turned out the light.

Flight Lieutenant Forbes.

He's the Adjutant, you know.

Oh, Matthew — you're going to be so proud.

Ellen, of course, will be impossible. My son, the Adjutant ... and why not Commanding Officer?

Typical of Ellen. No matter what Graeme does — no matter what he achieves, knock him down and make him pay for it. Your father would have been Air Marshal by now. What's wrong with you?

Nothing. Not any more.

Except ...

Miss Garter Belts.

To hell with Miss Garter Belts. I'll think about her tomorrow.

Tomorrow? You sound like Scarlett O'Hara.

I *am* Scarlett O'Hara. And I mean to get him back.

Rhett Forbes.

Mi laughed out loud.

Frankly, Michael, I don't give a damn!

Don't say that. Don't even joke about it. He's
coming back. He's already on his way.

Something struck the window.

What?

Something struck the window.

Mi got out of bed and crossed the floor — the planking cool
beneath her feet.

Perhaps the branch of a tree — and the wind ...

There isn't any wind.

Something struck the window.

There isn't any tree. No tree close enough.

Mi leaned down to the sill and looked out into the yard.

The moon was so bright she could count the roses in the rose bed.

"Michael?"

There was a man in uniform.

Something struck the window.

He was standing in the shadows — almost. Mi could see the
moonlit peak of his cap and the polished toes of his shoes.

"Michael?"

She didn't dare believe it.

"Graeme?"

"Yes. Come down."

Mi stepped back.

Come down.

She turned on the lamp and searched for her slippers under the bed.

Hurry.

Lying flat on the floor, she remembered she hadn't yet unpacked
the slippers and said: "to hell with them. It's Gray."

She stood up and put on her robe and collected her cigarettes
and went into the hall and came back into the room and looked at

her face in the mirror and picked up her brush and put it down without using it and dabbed some perfume behind her ears and left the room and went down the stairs.

A light was on in the hall for one of the guests who had requested it at dinner. *I'll be late, tonight,* and Mrs Mortson's *turn it off before you go upstairs ...*

Mi went over to the front door. She was shaking. She hadn't seen him since February, and here she was in nightdress and robe — barefooted and unkempt.

Well, at least he's not with Miss Garter Belts.

The door was not locked. It opened inwards — creaking — and the screen door opened outwards — also creaking.

From the porch, she could see some kind of automobile. A Ford convertible, the palest shade of blue in the moonlight.

In the moonlight, all the trees stock-still — not a breath of wind or breeze. In the moonlight, every blade of grass endewed — like a jewelled lawn.

In the moonlight, moving along the porch towards the corner beneath her bedroom — all the rocking chairs and tables standing waiting to be used — *how patient furniture is.*

"Graeme? Gray? Where are you?"

In the moonlight.

"Oh," she said. "Come here."

"No," he said. "Come here."

In the moonlight down the steps and across the lawn — the grass delicious, wet beneath her feet.

Graeme was standing, still in the shadow of the tree.

In the moonlight, Mi put out her hands. He did not come forward. This way, they remained for a moment — Mi in the moonlight, Graeme not.

"Hello," she said.

"Hello."

Mi's hands went back to her sides.

"I came to show you my new sleeves."

Mi saw the cuffs of his jacket, raised in the moonlight. Two white rings adorned them.

"Congratulations," she said. "You have the most beautiful sleeves I have ever seen."

Graeme laughed.

"Any chance I could look at them more closely?"

"Sure."

Mi went over through the moonlight into the shadows.

They embraced, but did not kiss.

He had not been drinking.

"I can only stay ten minutes," he said. "Ivan told me which window was yours."

"I'm glad your aim is still good. The lady next door would not have been amused. Stones at midnight — not her style."

Graeme took her hand.

"Is there somewhere we could sit?"

"Front steps."

Through the moonlight, back along the curve of the drive, but walking on the grass.

At the steps, they chose a place that was halfway up and sat.

"I feel like a kid," said Mi. "With a mad, romantic boyfriend."

Graeme said nothing.

So be it.

Mi said: "we love it here — but we won't be in your pocket."

Nothing. He was looking off — away from her, back at where he'd been standing in the shadows.

Mi said: "I'm proud of you, Gray. Being Adjutant and all — and your promotion."

She watched his profile — his ear, his nose — his lips in the moonlight. And the long-lidded, long-lashed eyes of a satyr — in which all the danger had died and all the laughter faded. Wary now — and weary.

Say something. Please.

No.

"When can I see you — officially?" she said. And smiled. But he didn't see.

"Sunday," he said. "There's a buffet dinner every Sunday night in the Officers' Mess."

"Can Matthew come?"

"Of course."

For a moment, they were silent — listening to the frogs and crickets — all the night sounds down by the river — over under the trees — in the shadows — in the moonlight.

"I'd better go," said Graeme.

He did not stand up.

Mi said nothing.

Finally, Graeme got to his feet and went down onto the path below her.

"I'll see you Sunday," he said. "Good night."

Mi did not rise.

She watched him turn and walk away — her mad, romantic boyfriend fading with him.

"Good night," she said — in a whisper.

He backed the car all the way to the gate — turned at the road and drove away.

All this way, not to tell me. All this way not to speak.

Oh, well. She sighed. I've seen his stripes.

My striped, mad boyfriend. Mute.

Then she got up and went in. She didn't want whoever it was who would be returning late to find her there in her nightgown, in her bathrobe, barefoot, halfway up the steps — as if she had lost her way. Being wayward — in the moonlight.

11th July, 1942

Two of the other guests at The Willows were what Matthew called *Muscle Men*. On the Friday, just before dinner, Mister Mortson had asked for their help in getting the steamer trunk into the house and up the stairs.

The two men were with the local Hydro crew, where they worked as tree-cutters. One of them had already been to the war and back and the other was too old to go. The younger man — whose name was Alvin Speaks — had been wounded in some way that was never mentioned, though you could see the pain of it in his eyes from time to time. Strangely, for a man called *Speaks*, he hardly spoke at all. The older man was Alex Ross and he and Alvin shared a room at the farthest end of the hall from Matthew and Mi.

In between, there was a nurse, whose name was Rose Walter. *Call me Miss Rose,* she had said when they were introduced. *Walter is a man's name.* Later she would tell Mi: *soon as I was old enough to know this, I took an instant dislike to it. All my life I've been* Miss Rose *and I intend to keep it that way.*

Mi was tempted to say: *yes, sir.* Also, to salute. But she resisted. There was not an ounce of humour in Miss Rose — not even of amusement. When Mi explained that her own name was Michael, Miss Rose said only: *I see,* as if she was saying: *that explains it, then.*

The Mortsons' bedroom was at the top of the stairs and beside the stairs, across the hall, there was an empty room reserved for a certain *Mrs Delaney,* who would return next week. *She's got them Very Close Veins you hear about,* Mrs Mortson explained. *She's into the hospital now, where God-knows-what's been done to fix 'em.*

Next door to Mi was Nella Mott, a wisp of a woman who painted wildflowers in water-colours and who spoke entirely in whispers. Miss Rose was not fond of Nella Mott. *She spends too much time in the bathroom, ignoring the needs of others,* she said. Mi rather liked her. She was genuinely sweet and wide-eyed, curious and informative. Her pictures were exquisite, filled with mood and character. Each of the flowers was an individual in an individual, identifiable place — not just a portrait of *a buttercup, a violet, a prim-rose.* Mi was determined that before the summer was out she would own one.

In the mornings, Mrs Mortson fed her husband and the Hydro men before the rest of the house was even awake. Alex and Alvin were given sandwiches and soup in black metal boxes and Thermos bottles and, six days a week, they drove away in their truck at seven. Saturdays, they got off early and Sundays, after sleeping in, they went to church.

Miss Rose was always first in the bathroom and first at table. *First in everything,* Mi would tell Eloise, *but first and foremost, a pain in the behind.* She tried to run all their lives and did everything but post house-rules to enforce her will. Her schedule was paramount — *lives depend on it* — and she told them all when to eat — when to go to bed — and when to use the bathroom. The house itself seemed to sigh with relief when she banged its door and was gone.

"Where does she work?" Mi wanted to know.

"Over to the Royal Victoria," Agnes Mortson told her.

"A hospital?"

"In Trenton, yes. Miss Rose is in the Crazy Wing."

Mi had to smile. *No wonder Miss Rose wants every ounce of order she can find.*

On the Saturday morning, while Matthew explored the barn with Hunter, the dog, Mi finished their unpacking and held a dress parade in front of the full-length mirror attached to the armoire. *Sunday Buffet in the Officers' Mess — and all those other wives, including ...*

"Wear the blue."

"I beg your pardon?"

"Wear the blue one."

It was Nella Mott. She was standing with her painting basket and her camp stool in the hall.

"Good morning, Miss Mott."

"Good morning. I do hope you don't mind my watching — but I was passing and ..." She stepped into the doorway and smiled. "I'm like a child with my nose up against the window-pane when it comes to clothes. I never have the opportunity to wear pretty things myself, but I love a chance to see them. Do wear the blue. It's so becoming."

Mi went back to the bed and exchanged the dress in her hand for the one suggested. It had now been restructured twice. Blue crêpe that hung against her body like a dream. Graeme had never seen this version, which had no back at all, to speak of.

"You will be the belle of the ball," said Nella Mott. "It is simply exquisite."

"It's not a ball," Mi said. "Unfortunately. It's just a buffet dinner."

"With your husband?"

"Yes. In the Officers' Mess."

"Wear the blue."

"And which shoes?"

Mi exposed the shoes displayed on the floor of the armoire.

"The blue-and-white," said Nella Mott. "Open blue toes, white heels. So handsome."

"In the evening?"

"It is a *summer* evening, Mrs Forbes. A summertime buffet — and all the men in summer uniform. You must carry something light and airy — a chiffon scarf, if you have one. You will look as if you have just arrived in the Bay on your private yacht and been delivered in an open *sports-coupé*. Those shoes, with their open toes — that dress, with its daring cut — the very essence of a summertime occasion."

Mi turned away. How sad this little woman was — standing there in her running shoes and her painter's smock, daydreaming yachts and motorcars and chiffon scarves, with her hair square-cut like a child's and her wide-brimmed summertime hat, with its faded ribbon tied beneath her chin.

"Sometime," Mi said, "you and I must go into town for dinner, Miss Mott. We will make a fashion show. And you will be my guest. I will not take *no* for an answer."

"Oh, Mrs Forbes — I couldn't."

"Yes, you could — and *will*." Mi turned and smiled. "Dinner for two in the dining-room of The Green Parrot. And we will dress to kill."

"The Green Parrot! Dressing to kill! Oh, my heavens!" Nella put her free hand over her mouth.

"So — it's a date?"

"Dear me! A date."

"Yes?"

"Why, yes — I would be delighted to accept, Mrs Forbes — and I shall live in keen anticipation."

Nella hovered in the doorway.

"I must go now," she said. "This is my day for bulrushes."

"Have a good time."

"I will. I will. There's a boat, you know."

"No, I didn't know."

"Yes. A rowboat. Called *The Bluebell*." Nella brightened. "Isn't it wonderful? Your blue dress — your blue shoes — my blue smock. And now, *The Bluebell*! It is one whole day of blue!"

Mi watched her vanish in the mirror.

One whole day of blue.

Still people full of wonder, she thought. *Full of wonder, full of hope. Living their lives in keen anticipation.*

Mi felt a wave of shame.

I have been living my life as though it was entirely devoid of wonder — and of hope. And I have no right. I have no right.

> *Wear the blue.*

Yes. And that new Elizabeth Arden lipstick. *Vibranté.*

Me and Irene Dunne.

12th July, 1942

Sunday, at four o'clock, Mi finished her hair and blotted her lips. She had saved a pair of silk stockings in a shade that Graeme particularly liked and she wore her trademark perfume — *Bois des îles*. Now, she placed a hand-towel over her head and drew on the dress. The feel of its descent past her hips made her shiver. When all was done, she stood away and looked at herself in the mirror.

> *Good shoulders, Mi.*

Like a dancer, Gray always says.

Said.

The dress was cut and draped in the shape of a shell, *good exposure front and back!* The blue was a perfect match for her eyes. *Mi-blue*, Eloise called it. *Mi-blue heaven* — grinning.

> *You look stunning.*

Yes — and I'd better!

Mi had thought about Sue Anne Howard all afternoon, dreading the meeting that might take place that night and equally dreading the thought that Sue Anne Howard would not be there at all. *It's time we saw each other face to face.*

Henry Mortson had kindly offered to drive them to the Air Base in his truck.

At 5:45, when Mi and Matthew came out onto the porch, Nella Mott was sitting in one of the rocking chairs.

"Good evening, Mrs Forbes. Matthew," she said, and stood up. "I wanted to wish you well — and I brought you this ..."

Mi was just at the edge of the steps. Nella came forward and handed her a tissue-paper package — flat and light as a feather. "I keep it as a memento of my mother," she said. "But you may use it this evening."

Mi pulled the paper aside to find a pale blue, folded cloth — and when she lifted it and shook it out, it proved to be a chiffon scarf.

Nella was smiling.

Mi leaned forward and kissed her. "I shall take special care of it. Thank you."

"Do have a lovely time," Nella said, and took back the tissue paper. "You are the very picture of enchantment."

"Thank you again. We'll tell you all about it in the morning."

"Yes, please. Everything you ate and what everybody wore."

"Every last crumb and every last stitch. Good evening, Miss Mott."

"*Bonne chance! Au revoir!*"

Matthew had to help Mi into the cab of the truck. It was some way up for someone in high heels. Then Matthew climbed in after her and slammed the door.

"Door'll fall off, you bang it like that," said Henry Mortson.

"Yes, sir. Sorry."

"Off we go, then."

Mi waved the scarf out the window and Nella Mott waved back.

"Must be something in the air," said Henry. "I never heard that woman speak more'n two words. Then she goes spoutin' off in languages!"

At the gates, there was a Guard House. Henry was not allowed to take the truck onto the base, so Mi and Matthew thanked him for his trouble and got down onto the road.

"You want a ride home, you call."

Mi nodded. "I'm hoping my husband will steal a car and bring us back. But thanks for the offer."

Henry turned the truck and drove off.

"We're here for the buffet dinner," Mi told the Corporal on duty. "I'm Mrs Graeme Forbes and this is our son, Matthew."

"Yes, ma'am. You're on the list. You may pass."

"Thank you."

Mi and Matthew moved towards the personnel gate, but ten seconds later Mi was back.

"We don't know where to go," she said.

"Keep on past the barracks on your right until you come to the corner of the Parade," she was told. "Turn left. Ignore the first building you pass — take the second. Once you're inside, someone will direct you."

"Thank you."

They set off again. The parade ground was immense. The barracks were immense. Four white buildings, each four storeys high. The sky was immense — spread out above them, emptied of aeroplanes. One lone gull was flying there — and not a cloud in sight.

Now, having turned the corner and having passed the building they were to ignore, they saw a water tower, painted red and white, and the tropical pallor of what they would learn to call *The Admin Building*.

"So," said Mi. "We're here."

Any minute, we'll see him.

"You ready?"

Matthew looked up at the wide expanse of windows on either side of the door before them. It was not his favourite kind of architecture. Too much like school.

I am Richard Hannay, facing the thirty-nine steps ... I am David Balfour in the tower ... I am Sydney Carton, climbing to the guillotine.

"Shall we?" said Mi.

"Yes." *I am Matthew Forbes, and I am going to see my father.*

Mi took his arm and they went up.

A dark-haired young man in a white jacket directed them to the far end of the corridor. An open doorway — seemingly a mile away — spilled its light towards them, laying down a blinding path along the floor.

"We should have worn our sunglasses," Mi said.

Matthew felt quite at home. The smells in the corridor reminded him of school — antiseptic, waxen, male. Also the smells of pencils and paper — books and ink and the smells of cabbage salad and hard-boiled eggs. Mi smelled none of this. For her, the corridor was redolent of apprehension — almost electric with it.

She had worn a shoulder bag woven of straw — the straw dyed blue — just big enough for cigarettes, matches, lipstick and hand-kerchief. She had tied Nella Mott's chiffon to the shoulder end of the strap, so it fell down either side of her arm. *My wing.*

At the doors, the light was almost palpable. The anteroom was empty, except for a long, narrow table covered with officers' caps, all lying right side up — one of them Graeme's.

Mi said: "when we go in, we'll let him come to us. Okay?"

Matthew nodded. They went through all the way to the mess, where they were assaulted by a chattering of voices, sounding like a flock of geese.

Mi chose a position dead centre on the north wall and, from there, they stood gazing over the backs of the chairs and sofas, past the tables and table lamps all the way to the farthest end of the room, with its bandstand raised a foot above the floor and the silent piano — waiting to be claimed. Beyond this, doors stood open giving a view of terrace and of tennis courts. Along one side of the room, trestles had been set with boards and the boards spread over with white linen cloths. A myriad of salads, breads and cold-cuts were displayed on these with bowls of peonies and tall, wobbly piles of plates and squat glass jugs of lemonade and apple juice.

Way off down the room, a shipwreck of men had washed ashore on an archipelago of women — all the men in pale khaki uniforms

— all the women Sue Anne Howard in a Paris dress. Or so it seemed to Mi. Each island of women was completely encircled and all she could see of the men was their backs.

Rising as a single island — rather like England and Scotland — the wife of the Commanding Officer stood in lonely splendour, surveying the archipelago in the manner of the Mother Country regarding its colonies. It was her job to chaperone these events and she did so with cool reserve. Over a full-length gown, she wore a tartan throw — England and Scotland, indeed.

"There he is," said Matthew.

Graeme's unmistakable shoulders were halfway along the route to the bar.

"Shall I get him?"

"No. He knows we're coming. Wait."

Graeme, having paused only briefly at one of the islands, had reached the bar and was turning away from it with glass in hand — a highball, dark as amber.

Mi closed her eyes and took a deep breath.

"Now?" said Matthew.

"No." Mi was resolute. "We're waiting for him here."

She adjusted a shoulder strap.

Graeme was looking at his watch.

At least he's wondering where we are ...

Gray?

Sipping his drink, he looked straight at her.

Telepathy.

He lowered the glass.

Would he put it aside?

No.

He began to move in their direction — nodding and smiling.

The old smile. Almost.

Mi smiled back.

Fifteen feet. Ten feet. Five.

She squared her shoulders.

Graeme said: "Matthew." Still smiling, his eyes on Mi.

"Hi, Dad."

"Mi."

"Gray."

He took her hand and leaned forward. She could hear the ice cubes shifting in his glass. He kissed her.

"Good to see you."

Mi stood back, silenced.

Graeme held up the glass and toasted her.

"Iced tea," he said.

Mi said nothing.

"Happy landings." Graeme drank and, turning, reached for Matthew's shoulder. "What would you like? There's lemonade over there."

"Thanks."

Matthew crossed the room, relieved and happy. Relieved that his father hadn't kissed him, and happy because his father was sober. There was also an edge of disorientation in all of this. Matthew had not seen Graeme in the flesh for such a long time that his father's age had been divorced from his person. The only image Matthew had of him was the one he had imprinted from the photographs at school. *Older than me, but younger than himself.*

Matthew filled a glass with lemonade, deciding he would leave his parents alone for a moment. *All that mushy stuff has to happen —* deeply embarrassing — *and all that other stuff I don't want to know —* some other woman Mi had talked about with Eloise. *Kids aren't supposed to understand these things — but we do. We understand every-thing. Other women. Everything.*

Matthew had once discovered a photograph of Graeme standing on the dock at Shanty Bay, wearing his bathing suit, arms akimbo, head thrown back in the sun. This picture rested, framed in silver, on the dressing-table of Mrs Porter — *Sylvia* — once his mother's friend. This had been just before the war. Matthew was eight. He was visiting Steven Porter, then a school chum in Miss Bransby's class. They sometimes stayed overnight in one another's houses.

Sylvia Porter was the only woman Matthew knew, besides his Grandmother Fulton, who was divorced. He didn't mind her, so long as she was playing Steven's mother. In that capacity, Sylvia could be a lot of fun — providing them with home-made hot dogs, just like the ones at the Ex, and letting them sit up late to hear "The Shadow" on the radio. But when she wasn't playing Steven's mother, she went out dancing with other people's husbands. Including Graeme. More than likely. Why else have his picture on her dressing-table? Also — why else hide it, next time Matthew came to stay overnight? Gone — until he saw it half-exposed in the dressing-table drawer.

Matthew had felt no guilt about invading Sylvia Porter's privacy — other people's bureau drawers were part of the treasure hunt involved in finding out who other people were. Still — he never told Mi what he'd found. And certainly not his father, though it grieved him not to be able to say: *I know.*

Now, his parents had wandered off without him — just as he'd hoped they would — and they would talk about this other *other* woman — and his father would lie and his mother would pass the lie on to Matthew: *everything's all right, now,* she would tell him. *Everything's fine.*

The way it always is — when it's not.

And yet ...

He isn't drunk. He looks okay. And he didn't kiss me.

Then Matthew went to look for Ivan Henderson.

Mi was introduced to the C.O. — *Group Captain Eugene Barker, D.F.C.* This was how she would describe him to Eloise: *wonderful man! Heroic. Moustache. Hardly any hair and a heavenly way with women — courteous, charming — just the right amount of flirting — you'll adore him!*

She and Graeme also bumped into Roy at the bar, when they were getting Graeme's second glass of iced tea and Mi's first martini and, later still, when they were filling their plates at the buffet tables. Graeme introduced her to some of the other men he worked with, and to their wives. It was here that Matthew rejoined them. He wore his first long trousers — white — and his red St Andrew's blazer. Graeme winked at him. "You look like me," he said.

No, I don't. Matthew looked away.

When they were all seated, Roy beside them, Mi was acutely aware this was the first occasion in over a year when she and Graeme and Matthew had all been together.

And Bonnie. Then.

Now, it's coming around again. The time of her death, one year ago tomorrow. Roy was there, too, that day.

Mi looked at Graeme and found herself suddenly thinking: *I want another baby.*

And you would be its father — all your running behind you — and all our lives in front. One more baby — Bonnie Renata — to keep us all alive. Please.

"You want some more iced tea?" she said.

Graeme nodded. "Matthew can get it."

Matthew started to rise.

"No. Sit. I'll do it." Mi touched Graeme's shoulder. "I'd like to."

She set down her plate and picked up her glass and Graeme's glass. "Roy?"

Roy shook his head and Mi went out into the room at large, like the heroine in a crowd scene — every eye fixed on her every move — the woman in the Mi-blue dress with its cleavage and back like inverted scallop shells and her swan's wing floating in the air behind her. *Who can she be, but the Belle of the Ball?*

I haven't felt like this in twenty years, she thought — *when I was seventeen and the other war was over and the whole wide world was my oyster and it gave me pearls.*

Matthew had seen Ivan Henderson coming out of a room that was not quite halfway along the corridor. His first reaction was to call out *hello*, but he couldn't remember Ivan's rank. Matthew watched with growing disappointment as his father's room-mate — wearing a short leather jacket — walked in the opposite direction, turned the corner and disappeared.

He's gone to ride his motorcycle, Matthew decided — not quite sure why this angered him.

He came to the doorway from which Ivan had emerged. The door was open. Matthew looked in. Windows faced the parade ground, lit now with evening light. Ivan was walking straight across the centre of it towards the gates.

Matthew went in.

It's my father's room. I'm allowed.

There were two beds, two bureaus and two chairs. *Like the pre-fects' room at school.* Also a desk in front of the windows and, on the desk, some books and papers. Nothing of fiction — only manuals and lists. The beds had cotton coverlets — sandy-coloured, with orange threads — and beside them, tables, each with a ticking clock.

Matthew stood in the centre of the room and turned in all directions. With some relief, he saw another door to the left of one of the beds. *The bathroom.* He needed desperately to pee.

Beyond the door, there was a sort of dressing-area. In spite of his need, he paused to switch on a light and to open one of the cupboards.

Dad. There's his old blue golf shirt.

He closed that door and opened the other.

Ivan.

Pee first.

Matthew went on through to the bathroom, switched on its lights and lifted the toilet seat.

While he went, he looked around him.

Dad must hate it. No tub. Just a shower.

He finished, did up his buttons and flushed the toilet.

Wash your hands.

No.

He inspected Ivan's shaving things and his father's nail clippers. Picking up Ivan's shaving brush, he "lathered" his face in the mirror. *Some day.*

What's that?

Some kind of medicine. Not his dad's. Ivan's. *Codeine.* The name meant nothing. He shook the bottle. Pills.

He smelled his father's shaving cream and smiled. *Home.* Ivan's shaving cream was different. Strangely medicinal. Matthew put it down — picked up and smelled the soap — made a face and went back into the dressing-room.

Ivan's cupboard was mostly uniforms, like his father's. Winter and summer — blue and tan — light and heavy. They smelled of cleaning fluid mostly and, very faintly, of something else Matthew could not identify.

There was a cardigan — black — and a dressing-gown — black — and a pair of leather trousers. Also black.

Matthew had never seen leather trousers.

He ran his fingers over the legs and the palms of his hands across the seat. Cool. And oddly unnerving. The flies had large, hard metal buttons. Cold. Matthew tried to imagine wearing the trousers and doing them up. Impossible. Your fingers would break.

He turned out the lights and went back into the bedroom. In his father's top drawer, hidden under a pile of fresh white hand-kerchiefs, he found *those balloons again*. He wasn't sure what they were for, but he'd seen one once in the park and had picked it up. This was on a day when there were several older children playing there and one of them had told him to throw it away.

It's just a balloon.

No, it's not! It's something dirty belonging to some man and you're not to play with it!

This had been before the war and the girl who had said this to him had been angry with him. Or so it seemed. She had raised her voice and given him a push. Annalise Cooper.

Matthew closed his father's drawer and went to Ivan's bureau.

Would Ivan have balloons?

No.

Matthew was disappointed, having thought he would steal them because Ivan had gone alone to ride on the motorcycle.

What Ivan did have was underwear and handkerchiefs and socks. Matthew smelled the underwear and thought he had never smelled anything so clean or seen anything so white.

We should have worn our sunglasses, Mi had said.

The shirts in the lower drawers were all the same. Blue and tan and boring. In the bottom drawer, some sweaters. Nothing else. No secrets. *Nothing dirty belonging to a man.* Nothing tucked between the shirts or rolled up in the socks. Just Ivan's clothes.

Matthew inspected the top of the bureau. Brushes to smell, a comb to hold over his upper lip like Hitler's moustache and only a single photograph in a frame.

Matthew stared.

Ivan, dressed in the black leather jacket and trousers, standing beneath a palm tree with his *second greatest love.* The Harley.

He wore no hat and there was no one else in the picture. Only Ivan and the motorcycle — gleaming, both of them — shining and polished in the sun.

Under a palm tree.

Somewhere far away.

Matthew turned out the lamps and left the room. He did not go back to the mess at once. Instead, he went along the corridor in Ivan's footsteps, out through the doors and down all the way to the drive.

There was the parade ground.

Matthew stood at its edge.

The sun was lower now, and all the shadows longer.

Far, far away, he could hear the sound of a motorcycle engine — revving.

There was not a soul in sight but one lone man, who stood in his undershirt against the sill of an open window high in the barracks.

Smoking a cigarette, he was utterly still and gazing out at the evening light.

As Matthew watched, the man leaned forward and dropped his cigarette to the ground below. He watched it falling all the way down. When it landed, he took a step backward, leaving the window open and empty.

Matthew listened.

The revving motor had been kicked and gunned into action. The sound of it was now so distant, it was almost silent. It whispered *Ivan* — and was gone.

Matthew turned and went back up the steps and through the doors and down the corridor.

At the bar, having ordered iced tea for Graeme and for herself, Mi stood watching a table of six young men and three young women. *So god-damned full of life — all that beautiful skin and hair — clear-eyed and unafraid ...*

"Mrs Forbes?"

It was the barman.

"Yes?"

"Your tea."

"Thank you."

Mi was about to cross the room when she heard the words *Sue Anne.*

She turned. One of those women laughing at the nearby table must be her. Sue Anne Howard. But which?

"Anybody want to go out on the terrace — catch a breath of air?"

A girl in her early twenties was pushing back her chair and rising. Both the other women and one of the men said: "sure."

They, too, got up and started for the doors. The other men stayed put.

Mi had to know.

She delivered the tea to Graeme and said: "I'm just stepping out for a moment. Won't be long."

As she made her way towards the doors, a man at the piano was playing "You'll Never Know" — and Mi thought: *yes, I will.*

The group she had followed were standing at the farthest end of the terrace leaning along the railing like passengers on a ship. Mi stood close enough to hear, but not to look as if she was eavesdropping.

One of the women was standing apart. Mi thought she looked familiar, but did not know why. Pretty and serious. Thoughtful. Sad. She was blonde and blue-eyed. Classic. Her hair was relatively short and brushed away from her face. She wore a plain cotton dress — yellow, verging on apricot. Its belt and collar were white.

Where have I seen her? That face — that demeanour — almost — something thwarted, forgotten, held back. There had once, Mi was certain, been energy there — a sort of keen *I'm dancing! Watch me!* playfulness — gone, now.

Why do I remember her?

Introduce yourself.

Don't be ridiculous. What would I say?

I like your dress.

Please!

Okay. What about, I hate *your dress?*

I think not.

Mi took a look at the other two women. *They were more the Sue Anne type. Much less fragile. Giggly — light-headed girls with Andrew Sisters hair and swingtime dresses — much too short and far too revealing.*

Ankle-strap shoes — a dead giveaway. One of them a redhead, the other brunette — and wild, crazy laughter every two minutes. Probably telling risqué jokes. That's done a lot, these days — women telling men dirty jokes. Women saying shit.

You say shit.

Not in public.

The young man with them was relatively handsome. Boyish, with an athletic body — his face a mass of freckles. Mi could imagine someone calling him Sandy.

Sandy and Sue Anne.

It can't be the redhead. She's just too silly for words. Graeme might be smitten with her for five minutes — but no longer. *Wham-bam and thank you, ma'am.* That sort of thing — but not a steady interest.

And the other? The brunette?

Great legs. Graeme's passion. A little more subdued. Nice figure. Maybe intelligent. I doubt it. Look at the eyes. And not a pensive bone in her body. It could be her. But what does she have to offer? Nothing that I don't have. Except ...

The brunette turned and looked at Mi, but there was not a trace of interest in her expression.

Yes? Except what?

I don't know — that *je ne sais quoi* that makes two people click.

Click?

Yes. Click.

People click in different ways, for different reasons, Mi. She doesn't have to click with him the way you do.

Did.

The brunette turned sideways and spoke to the redhead. The redhead looked at Mi, but only briefly. Something was said that Mi could not hear.

Maybe my hair looks funny ...

I wouldn't worry.

But what if one of those is Sue Anne?

Go up and ask. It's the only way you'll find out.

I can't.

Sandy, the redhead and the brunette were leaving. They walked past Mi as if she wasn't there, ignoring her completely. And no one's name had been mentioned. This meant Mi would have to ask Roy, and she didn't want to do that. It would expose her vulnerability and, above all, Mi did not want to be seen as *the poor wife* — as being a victim. That Graeme's infidelity was known to Roy at all was bad enough.

She went and stood at the railing where the others had been when she came out. Tennis courts. Trees. A sports field. The Bay. From the mess Mi could hear music. A band had joined the pianist. People would now be dancing. It was getting dark, and time for all good girls to go inside ... *Michael Maude! Michael Maude!*

"Sue Anne? You coming in?"

This was Sandy — standing in the open doorway.

The one remaining girl — the blue-eyed blonde — was still on the terrace, leaning on the other railing, looking off towards sunset.

"No," she said. "Later."

Mi did not know what to do. As Sandy left and Sue Anne turned again to the far horizon, Mi got out her cigarettes and lighted one. *She doesn't know who I am,* she thought. *It can't do any harm. I'll stay here till she leaves.*

She regretted having chosen to drink iced tea. Another martini would be welcome, right now.

So. That's Sue Anne Howard.

Her head was still turned away — and Mi had the impression she might be weeping.

And why not. She's losing Graeme.

Is she?

You're here, my dear. You are here and you are Graeme's wife.

What else is new?

"Excuse me."

Sue Anne had turned. And had been weeping. *Yes.*

"Do you think you could let me have a cigarette?"

"Of course."

As the girl approached, Mi caught a whiff of her perfume. That, too, was familiar.

"There you go."

Sue Anne Howard accepted the cigarette and put it, trembling, to her lips. As Mi struck the match and held it for her, she could see the patterns of Sue Anne's tears.

"Thank you."

Sue Anne settled with her back against the railing near Mi.

"I don't smoke very often, but ..." She looked away. "I'm having such a bad time."

"I'm sorry."

No you're not.

"My husband ..."

Go on. Tell me.

"He was killed out there. Learning how to fly."

I know. Eloise told me.

"He was just a boy. Billy. We'd only been married three months. Three and a half."

"I'm sorry."

Sue Anne tried to laugh.

"I was pregnant. Wouldn't you know it? Pregnant. And I'd come down here to live. We were married here. And had the craziest honeymoon. They wouldn't let him go away, so we went and stayed in The Green Parrot. You know it?"

"Yes."

"It snowed." She looked away. "I love the snow. I love to see it falling. You know? How it just sort of glides — just sort of floats down through the air like bits of paper lace ..."

"Yes."

"And I was so happy. It was like a gift — a wedding gift — the world all white for our wedding cake." She smiled. "I shouldn't tell a stranger this — but you know what we did?" She giggled. "We opened our windows wide — that night — wide as wide could be and we ..."

Yes?

"... we climbed out naked through the windows and put our arms out, just like this ..." She demonstrated. "Just like this and stood there on the roof and let it snow all over us. All over us. All ..."

Mi was silent. Watching. Enchanted and afraid. This girl — this child — was her enemy — but all she wanted to do was hold her in her arms and comfort her.

Don't.

Don't worry. I won't.

"Have you ever?"

"What?"

"Stood naked in the snow."

Mi thought about it.

Laugh. You have to.

"Not on my wedding night." She smiled.

Sue Anne smiled back.

"I feel better now."

"Good. I'm glad." And then: "your baby? When will it be born?"

"It won't."

"I don't understand."

And you, the mother of three dead children ...

"I had ... I had an accident."

You fell downstairs.

"I fell downstairs."

Mi closed her eyes. In her mind, it snowed. That was it. Snow and a blonde young woman eating the flakes from her husband's shoulder. February. Graeme impotent and, in the lobby of The Green Parrot, snow and Betty Grable. Mi opened her eyes. *Not Betty Grable any more. Never was. It was all a game — and one of them playing it, died.*

"You'll meet somebody," she said, "and you will marry. There will be other children ..."

"I've already met somebody."

I know.

"But ..."

He's married.

"... he's married."

"That happens. You'll get over it."

"Will I?"

"Yes. At least, I hope so. For your sake." *And for mine.* "My parents were divorced. They were never happy again. It ruined my father's second marriage. My mother died broken."

"Well ..."

Sue Anne looked at the sky.

"I guess we'd better go in," she said. "Thanks for your company. And for listening."

No names were mentioned. None was needed. *It's best,* Mi thought, *that she doesn't know who I am. After all, we've never been introduced. It wouldn't be proper.*

17th July, 1942

At six o'clock the following Friday, Graeme stood before his bureau, brushing his hair.

Dad gave me these.

"A man's brushes should last him a lifetime," Tom had said.

Dying. He was dying. Dying and knew he was dying. God — the burden of it — one whole year of knowing.

Tom Forbes had died in 1917. Ian Forbes in 1918. When Tom laid out his male possessions, he gave his brushes, his cuff-links and studs to Graeme and assigned his watch to Ian. When Ian was killed, Ellen Forbes had kept the watch. Plus its chain and fob. *Mine*, she had said. The fob — an amethyst — had been her gift. And a note long ago destroyed which Graeme had found and burned. *My dear, my dear, my dear one — our stone and us, forever.* She also kept Ian's medals and his wings. Kept them and enshrined them. Every day, she wound the watch and put it back in its glass case — not so much to look at as to hear. Time, while it must not be seen to pass, must be heard.

Time is a maniac, scattering dust,
And life, a fury slinging flame....

Or something.

A month after Tom's death, Ellen had a hundred copies of *In Memoriam* printed and bound in blood-red leather, all the pages edged in black. She had given them to friends, forced them on mere acquaintances, *so Tom will never be forgotten.* She posted them as far away as China, India and Scotland, with Tom's name and dates impressed in gold on the covers. When someone pointed out that

Tennyson had not been credited with writing the poem, Ellen said: *what does it matter? The words are what matter, and the words are there.*

Time is a maniac, scattering dust.

You're damn tootin', Mother! And fuck you, too.

Graeme set the brushes aside.

Tonight I'm going to scatter me some dust with Sue Anne Howard.

Of course, he hadn't told Mi. She was taking Matthew to the movies, anyway. What did it matter if he had the night off and might have joined them. *Sitting in the dark and watching* Pinocchio. *No thanks.*

He looked at Ian in his silver frame. Dashing, in his uniform. *That was the word for it.* Dashing. *People don't say that any more.*

Graeme looked at himself.

Maybe I'll grow a moustache. Like the C.O. Manly.

Ian's jacket was belted with leather. *Better looking than this damn thing. This damn thing only has a cloth belt — its pockets look as if they've been filled with sand. And I don't have any ribbons.*

Rat-a-tat-tat. The death of Richthofen. *Rat-a-tat-tat.* Errol Flynn in *The Dawn Patrol. Rat-a-tat-tat.* Ian Forbes receives the Military Cross. *Rat-a-tat-tat.* Graeme Forbes gets to fly a desk. *A goddamned, fucking, cock-sucking desk.*

Graeme squinted at his reflection.

I can't be thirty-nine. I don't look it. More like twenty-nine.

God, Ian — you were only nineteen. Going on twenty. Nineteen — going on twenty — and look at you. Dashing.

I bet you slayed the babes. Ian Forbes — Babe-slayer!

Shot down in flames.

Somewhere in France.

I've never even been to your grave. Mother went. Damn her. I was left in Paris with Isabel. Your bloody twin sister — and Mother wouldn't let her go. It's my death more than yours, *she said.* My death more than yours. *She actually said that.* Mine!

Like Dad. When Dad died. MINE!

MY DEAD — ONLY MINE!

Oh, Christ — now, I'm crying.

He opened his top drawer and got out a handkerchief.

You never saw me play. You never saw me run with the ball ... I never saw you fly. And I never saw your grave.

Nineteen.

I'm glad you don't know what I'm doing. Tonight. I'm going to some flea-bag tourist cabin and I'm going to screw a woman who isn't my wife. Not because I want to — but because I have to. I have to. It's all I have left ...

Ivan came in from the tennis courts. His shirt was soaking wet — but he was smiling.

"You should get out there. Chase the ball for a while. A few back-handed slammers and all your troubles are gone." He swatted Graeme's behind with his racquet. "All that sitting isn't good for you."

"I know that."

"You ever play?"

"Sure." A lie. Graeme had never touched a tennis racquet in his life.

"Well, anytime you want" — Ivan was pulling off his shorts — "I'd be happy to give you a workout."

"I don't need a workout. Thanks just the same."

"It was only an idea."

"I don't need your ideas."

"Well — I beg your pardon."

"And for Christ's sake put something around your waist. I don't need your dick in my face all the time."

Ivan said nothing and headed for the bathroom.

Graeme held the edge of the bureau — holding it so tightly his knuckles turned white.

I'm going to have a drink.

He looked up. There was his face.

How had he got there? All the way to *I'm going to have a drink.*

I'm going to have a drink. Just like that — out of nowhere, without an ounce of warning.

There's that bootlegger. Calvino. We'll park and Sue Anne can go in …

Ivan came to the door with a towel held in front of him.

"Look, Graeme — I'm sorry, but I have to say this. What you're doing is not a good idea."

"What?"

"What you're doing, for Christ's sake. What you're going to do tonight."

"How the hell do you know what I'm going to do tonight?"

"Jesus, Gray. You must be some kind of rot-brained idiot. GO BACK TO YOUR WIFE!"

Graeme blinked.

"It's none of your business," he said.

"Yes, it is. You're my friend."

Graeme was amazed.

My friend?

Ivan said: "you're better than this, Gray. And Michael doesn't deserve it."

Graeme began to put things into his pockets. Cigarettes. Lighter. Handkerchief.

"Look — you don't have to do this! That girl can live without you. Your wife can't."

Graeme was silent. He looked at his fingernails.

Ivan said: "if you want, I'll call her. Tell her you can't come. We could go out together. Have dinner at The Green Parrot. Something."

"No thanks."

"Okay. All right. Go ahead. Be a pig."

Graeme turned away. Then back. "I'm not a pig," he said. But Ivan had gone and the shower was running.

Graeme picked up his cap from the bed, patted his pockets and left.

I'll tell her this is the last time.

I'll say: we can't do this any more.

I'll say: we've had a good time — but ...

No. I'll say: look — you can live without me, Sue Anne. But Mi can't.

Then I'll say: that's why I want the Scotch. One last toast — to one last time with you.

At the curb outside the building, Sue Anne was waiting in her car. A pale blue Ford, with the top down.

"Put it up, for God's sake," said Graeme. "Do you want everyone to know?"

19th July, 1942

On their second visit to the mess, Mi and Matthew walked. It took them half an hour. Mi wore flat-heeled shoes and carried her others in a cloth bag. Also in the bag was a jar of peanuts and two tins of sardines for Graeme.

Early evening along the road there was very little traffic. A farmer passed on his tractor. Another farmer passed with horses. Two trucks, one of them painted Air Force blue, and three civilian cars also went by. People waved or saluted. The farmer with the horses called out: "evening," and raised his hat.

The side of the road was sandy, dry, and its grass was brown — almost dead. Matthew saw a snake — it was green — but he said nothing. Mi did not like snakes. Matthew had held one once in the backyard at Crescent Road and had thought how lovely it was in its black and yellow skin, with its dry, cool belly passing between his fingers. *No,* Mi had said. *Not in the house.* It lived in the garden all that summer.

Matthew had brought a chocolate bar.

"Don't ruin your supper."

He ate it anyway. *Sweet Marie.*

At the gate, there was a blue convertible coming through. Mi knew whose it was. Matthew knew it was a 1939 Ford. Sue Anne Howard, wearing a scarf around her hair and also wearing sunglasses, stopped to speak to the guard on duty — laughed at something and drove away. Mi said nothing.

In the Admin Building, they went to Graeme's room, so that Mi could change her shoes.

Graeme was lying on his bed.

Mi said: "what's the matter? Are you tired?"

Graeme did not sit up. He lay with one hand over his eyes and said: "get out of here."

Mi said: "I beg your pardon?"

Graeme said: "women are not allowed in these quarters." His voice was as dead as his posture.

"I assumed because we were in this building ..."

"You assumed wrong. Get out." His hand went back to cover his eyes.

Mi said: "Graeme, please." She was thinking of Matthew. Graeme had not yet acknowledged his presence.

"Before you leave, tell me what time it is."

"Six-thirty."

"I'm not hungry."

"Well — we can't go in there alone, Graeme."

"Sure you can. You just can't come in here."

Matthew went and stood in the window, looking out. He had heard all this before — the tones of voice — the aggressiveness — the defensiveness. The war between his parents.

Mi said: "I brought you some peanuts and sardines."

"Unh-hunh."

"Where should I put them?"

"Bureau."

Mi took the jar and the tins out of the bag and set them beside Graeme's brushes. There was Ian. Smiling. A copy of the photograph Ellen had enshrined at Foxbar Road. Scarf. Wings. Propeller. Smiling. Dead.

Ignoring the invitation to leave, she sat on Ivan's bed and changed her shoes. As Matthew had often heard her do before, she became businesslike.

"Come on, Graeme. Up."

She stood up, herself.

"We can have a couple of drinks and some food and we'll go," she said.

"I'm not hungry."

"Graeme. Get up."

"LEAVE ME THE FUCK ALONE!"

Matthew cringed.

Mi said: "hello, Ivan."

Matthew turned.

Ivan Henderson was standing in the doorway. He was wearing tennis shorts and a white sweater. He carried a racquet and his pockets bulged with tennis balls.

"Hello."

"We were just going in to eat. Will you be coming?"

"No. I mean — I hadn't planned on coming. But ..."

"Please do. We hardly know each other — and I'm sure Matthew would like to hear more about the motorcycle. Wouldn't you, Mattie?"

Please don't call me Mattie.

"Yes."

There was a moment of silence. Of course, Ivan had heard what Graeme had said. He looked at Mi. She bit her lip and smiled.

Ivan blushed. Matthew was watching him. Something happened. Mi looked away. So did Ivan.

Graeme said: "I apologize for my wife's inappropriate presence."

Ivan said: "not to worry." Matthew could barely hear him. "I'll change and join you." Ivan set his racquet on a chair, emptied his pockets, went into the bathroom and closed the door.

Graeme sat up. He looked at Mi, whose back was to him — then at the floor.

"Great legs, eh?"

"Thank you," said Mi — and turned.

"I didn't mean you," Graeme said. Their eyes met. Mi turned back to the bureau.

Graeme stood up.

"Okay, then," he said. "Let's go."

He led them down the hall.

He had not yet spoken to Matthew.

Matthew sat with his plate balanced on his knees. He was eating stale potato salad.

"How would you like the surprise of your life?" Graeme said.

Matthew was not sure he was being spoken to. Graeme had set aside his half-finished plate of food and was nursing a glass of Scotch and water.

"Matt?"

Matthew looked up.

"How would you like the surprise of your life?"

"Now?"

"No. Tomorrow."

"What is it?"

"Dumbo. If I tell you, how can it be a surprise?"

"When, tomorrow?"

Graeme looked at Ivan. Ivan shrugged.

Graeme said: "you still in for this?"

"If you want to — sure." Ivan was sitting next to Matthew.

Graeme smiled. "So. What time?"

Ivan said: "let's say five o'clock."

"What's all this about," Mi asked.

"You'll see," said Graeme.

"Sounds mischievous to me," said Mi.

"Maybe."

"Am I included?"

"Sure." Graeme looked at Ivan, but he spoke to Mi and to Matthew. "There's a road running north and south to the east of The Willows. Know it?"

"Yes."

"Be there — on the road — at five tomorrow afternoon."

Matthew thought: *motorcycle. They're going to come on the motorcycle.*

"I don't understand," said Mi.

"Just be there. With Matt."

"All right."

"Okay, chief?"

"Yes," said Matthew.

"Surprise of your life, that's what. Surprise of your whole uneventful life."

Mi winced.

Graeme was smiling.

"What'll we wear?" she said. Half-facetiously — more to counter the meanness of Graeme's last remark.

"Clothes," said Graeme. He winked at Ivan. Ivan looked at his food.

Matthew thought: *I hope we don't have to do this every Sunday.*

At eight o'clock, Ivan drove them home in a station wagon. Nothing was said.

Graeme went to his room and ate both tins of sardines. Then he went back to the mess and ordered a double Scotch.

20th July, 1942

The road was in fact a track — perhaps laid down in early cattle drives and then made formal by the passage of carts and wagons. It was rutted and high-ridged — rolling off to either side into shallow ditches that in spring and autumn served as waterways. It ran up between the Bay and the highway in the south-east section of Henry Mortson's farm, where he maintained what he called his *ranch. Cattle gone over to the ranch,* he would say, meaning these coarse grass acres where the earth was too shallow to plough. A maple bush stood between them and The Willows — a woods through which Mi and Matthew walked at four-thirty on the Monday afternoon.

Hunter and Nella Mott more or less accompanied them — except that Hunter kept haring off after rabbits and Nella kept stopping to examine wildflowers.

The sky had nothing in it — not even birds. The sun had its place — due west — but only a fool would look at it. Because of the trees, its light was delivered in uneven strokes — some of them green and others dusty, where Hunter had gone running.

There was an animal path. Cow patties to avoid. Right at the centre of the wood, the cattle had made a wallow — all the detritus, leaves and last year's withered undergrowth, crushed to a powder and the earth exposed. It smelled of animals and sand and moss.

Hunter came loping. *Am I lost?*

Mi said: "why is it so quiet? All the aeroplanes have stopped."

Not that it was entirely silent. There were flies and mosquitoes — but, largely, it was as if there was no Air Base nearby, or a highway beyond the woods. No human beings. No human activity.

Nella caught up with them where the shade gave way to meadow-light. "Do you think they are here already," she said, "and are going to jump out at us?" She wore her summertime hat and had also brought her umbrella, which she called her parasol. It was black. Now, she raised it and started walking south towards the Bay.

"Could be," said Mi, and followed her.

Where the land gave way to the water, there were limestone outcroppings — and the track turned west towards The Willows. Matthew and Mi and Nella went and stood on the rocks. Hunter splashed into the shallows and lay down.

"Someone knows how to get cool," said Mi.

Matthew turned and looked along the track. It was almost straight as an arrow. "Wait," he said — and shaded his eyes.

"What?"

"*Wait!*"

Why?

Mi and Nella turned.

There was a sound.

What was it?

A truck? A car? A tractor?

The motorcycle.

Matthew was certain of it.

Wait.

All three faced the track.

Nothing.

Nothing but the noise increasing. Something — whatever — approaching.

Then it was there.

BANG!

An aeroplane with yellow wings.

Almost ground level, coming straight at them.

Nella ran from the rocks and fell to the ground.

Mi stepped down into the water. Hunter stood up and shook himself.

Matthew crouched.

What is happening?

The noise was deafening. The whole field — the whole sky — the woods — The Willows — the Bay — everything shouted.

All the grass was flattened — all the leaves on the trees were turned and the branches lifted.

WHOOM.

It was gone.

Out over the Bay, skimming like a yellow stone.

Mi climbed out of the water. Nella sat up. All four turned.

"What?"

"A Harvard."

"They might have killed us."

"They might have killed themselves."

The aeroplane was turning now — banking and turning — climbing. It flew up over them, flying north — its shadow flying under it along the track.

Hunter barked. Mi and Matthew and Nella watched.

The Harvard had all but disappeared. Its engine had left a residue of acidic exhaust. They could see the black and yellow shape climbing — disappearing — reappearing — turning.

"They're coming back."

"They seem very high."

They were. But only for seconds.

The surprise of a lifetime.

All at once, the Harvard tipped towards the earth.

No.

Don't.

What?

It fell — was falling — towards them — diving.

Don't, Ivan — Graeme. Don't.

The Harvard's fall was so steep, it seemed to want to plough the earth.

When it levelled — and it did — Matthew could see Ivan's face. And his father's. Graeme was yelling. It looked like *STOP!*

The aeroplane screamed.

Mi's hand went, automatically fisted, to her lips.

Nella whispered: "dear God in Heaven."

The Harvard swooshed out over the Bay again. It climbed while Ivan tipped and waggled its wings.

Farewell.

In seconds, it was gone.

Mi was out of breath.

Matthew stood and stared at the sky.

Hunter, baffled, lay on the grass — with his paws pointing at the empty Bay.

Nella said: "I think I would have preferred the motorcycle."

Walking back to The Willows, Mi said: "you realize they've broken every rule in the book."

"Yes," said Nella. "Except, they do that all the time."

"Dad and Ivan?"

"No, no. Everyone. All the young pilots. Roaring around the sky as if they were playing a game."

"Well, it's not allowed, whoever does it," said Mi. "We mustn't tell anyone."

"Quite right. I agree."

"Ivan could lose his wings. Graeme could lose his position," said Mi. Nella corrected her. "It's my understanding," she said, "that once you have gained your wings, they're yours for life. But Mister Henderson could be court martialed. Maybe even Mister Forbes."

"Dear Lord — whatever made them do it?"

"I thought it was terrific," said Matthew. "Wow!"

Nella said: "there's your answer, Michael." She was smiling.

22nd July, 1942

Nella was sitting in the back of *The Bluebell*. Matthew was rowing.
He wore a sun hat and shorts, the hat made of white cotton.

"Always cover the back of your neck," said Nella. "The back of
your neck is the nerve centre of the world. Did you know that?"

"No."

"In the sun, keep it covered. If you don't, you'll get sunstroke."

There was that man in the movie Four Feathers. *He went blind when
he lost his hat in the sun.*

"Will I go blind?"

"You could." Nella always played on the safe side.

"There's something else about the back of your neck," she said.
"You know how, when you go swimming and the water's terribly
cold, you just about go crazy trying to get in?"

"Yes. Pretty nearly all the time."

"Well — what you do is — scoop up some of the water in your
hand and pat it all along here." She demonstrated, patting the back
of her neck. "Or, you can use a handkerchief — the edge of a shirt
— a towel — any bit of cloth. You just dip it in the water and lay
it out right there. Back of the neck."

Nerve centre of the world.

"That way, you won't have a heart attack when you put the rest
of you into the water — because the rest of you has already
adjusted to the cold. Do you see?"

"Yes, ma'am."

"Science is wonderful. Knowing just that tiny little bit about
your body can save your life."

"Yes'm."

They were on the river, south of the barns, whose roofs they could see beyond the rushes. "It's a marsh, right here," Nella said. "More like a marsh than a river, though you can feel the current, of course. I do love it so. All these slender, tender reeds and rushes — water lilies — serpent's tongue. See there — the water lilies? Lotus flowers is what they are. And do you hear the blackbird singing? There. Just listen. Hear him?"

Yes.

"That is the red-winged blackbird — king of the marshlands. He's built his nest in there. Did you know that? Among the reeds."

No.

"Listen to him. There. He is saying: *this is me!* He is saying: *I am these reeds and rushes. I am this water — I am this marsh.* He is singing: *I am this place and this place is me.*" Nella shaded her eyes beneath the brim of her summertime hat. "That's pretty much what all birds sing," she said. "That and *I am here* and *where are you?* Isn't it wonderful? Isn't it just astonishing? That's what the geese are calling when they fly. Did you know that? Those heavenly flights, high up, of geese — in the autumn — in the spring. Those high, wide flights — those ..." Nella spread and lifted her wings to the sky. "And all that glorious noise they make? *I am here. Where are you?*" Her arms descended, one hand resting on her shoulder, while the other adjusted the fall of her smock so it covered her knees. "I do so wish I could be a bird. A bird or a reed or all this water ..." *Anything but what I am.*

She was silent for a moment and then she smiled. "Do you ever have such thoughts? Not to be who or what you are, but something — someone else?"

Richard Hannay. David Balfour. Sydney Carton.

"Yes."

"And if it was an animal you chose to be — which one?"

"A fox."

"A fox. Dear me. A fox doesn't live very long. All those dogs. And men with guns."

"But he's clever."

"Yes. Oh, yes. And beautiful. Have you ever seen a fox in the flesh?"

"No. In pictures."

"They're smaller than you might think. Sometimes, their tail is just as long as their body. Sometimes longer. It makes their enemies think they're huge — but they're not. They're just like *this*." She demonstrated. "Small and compact — neat as a pin. And they move like angels." Nella laughed. "In the wintertime, they move like small red angels — streaming over the snow, with messages from God ..."

Matthew stopped rowing.

They drifted.

He shipped the oars.

Nella looked down at her knees.

She blinked and drew her finger over her lips.

That man came back again last night.

Matthew was watching a pair of ducks with their young. Wood ducks. *The most beautiful plumage in the whole wide world,* Nella had said. *Caps of feathers — slicked back just as if they'd used a comb! The red-eyed wonders of the wild.*

Nella squinted at the water.

He was in her room again.

She looked at Matthew.

I don't think he knows.

Such a handsome young man. And dashing, in his uniform. Almost a gentleman — but not. Not quite. Polite enough, but … He rides a motorcycle.

Nella got out her sketchbook and her conté crayons and began to draw the ducks.

It's afternoons like this — these sultry, dangerous afternoons — when anything can happen.

Ivan's back was to her.

"I haven't anything with me," he said. "We must be careful."

Mi said nothing.

She was lying under the sheet, demure as a girl. She had undressed while he was down the hall in the bathroom.

Ivan was naked. The window was open, the curtains blowing.

He looks just like Graeme, Mi thought. *The way Gray looked when we were young. All those long, lean lines.*

The Victrola was open, its handle shining. They had been playing all the songs — sitting, chatting, Mi not even smoking. How could one know this was going to happen? Matthew was on the river with Nella Mott. It wasn't intentional. She hadn't sent him there. *Miss Mott took him — said to him:* would you be my oarsman? *Yes.*

My oarsman.

Ivan stood by the side of the bed.

They had been dancing. It was like a risqué novel, one of those books about daring romance. Heat. Two strangers. On a summer afternoon. In the movies, the violins would swell — their fingers would touch — he would draw her close — almost, not quite, an embrace — and they would dance. Dance, while the light around them turned them into silhouettes — two silhouettes — then one.

It wasn't meant to happen. No one intended it. I didn't. He didn't.

His hand was pressed, there — in the small of my back.

No more dancing.

We didn't move.

The music went on playing. "Two Sleepy People" — all the way to the end. And we ...

Just stood there.

Knowing. Beginning to know.

And parting.

He lifted the needle — stopped the record — set the arm in place.

Henry Mortson called to his cattle — somewhere off in the fields.

The dog barked. Hunter.

Henry Mortson and Hunter, wading through the tall grass. Matthew and Nella drifting on the river. An aeroplane.

Ivan had watched it through the ceiling, followed it all the way across the sky.

I said.

Nothing.

Nothing.

Nothing was said.

He began to undo his tie.

I began to undo my belt.

I said.

Nothing.

He turned. We saw each other's eyes.

He said: I'll be right back.

I said.

Nothing.

The door opened. The door closed. He was gone.

I could hear the taps.

I got undressed. Everything. But my slip. I laid it all — I put each piece — my dress — my bra — my pants — my garters — stockings — everything but my slip in the chair. There it is.

I've only ever known three men in all my life. Two before Graeme. And Graeme.

The life and times of Michael Maude Fulton.

Nothing, nothing, nothing.

Ivan pulled aside the sheet.

Mi could feel the heat of his body.

Henry Mortson was calling Hunter: "come now, laddy. Home."

Mi put her hand on the back of Ivan's head and drew him down.

Whatever happens now, I know what I am doing.

Not adrift any more. Not lost. Not lost, but found.

"I must go, now."

"Yes."

Ivan had risen and dressed. He was standing — awkwardly — in the middle of the room. Mi had put on her Japanese kimono and was sitting on the bed.

"I'll be flying tomorrow. And the next day. And the next."

"Yes."

"I don't quite know what to say ..."

"Don't say anything."

He took his cap from the top of the bureau and held it in his hands.

"Perhaps next week."

"You promised Matt you'd take him out on the motorbike."

"Yes. And I will, but don't say *motorbike*. It's a *cycle*."

"Sorry." She looked at him. "Boys," she smiled, "have to get the words right. Yes?"

"Yes." He was smiling, too.

They were silent. Ivan crossed the room and touched Mi's shoulder. She put her hand on top of his and said: "you'd better go. They'll all be coming back any minute. Think what Miss Rose would say."

"Yes."

"Goodbye."

"Yes."

The door opened.

It closed.

Goodbye.

Yes.

Goodbye.

24th July, 1942

"When are we going to see Dad?"

"I don't know."

"Why are we here, if we never see him?"

"We see him Sundays."

"Yes, but ..."

"Sunday."

They were sitting side by side in rockers on the porch. The sun was in the willow trees, starting its slow descent. Hunter was lying flat out, asleep on the boards beside them.

The screen door whined and banged.

It was Miss Rose, carrying the evening paper. Mi and Matthew knew, now, not to speak to her unless she spoke to them. Just last week, she had come home from the Crazy Wing so tense, she behaved as if someone had handed her the entire war and had said: *here — deal with this.*

All the doors had banged — her car door — the screen door — her bedroom door — the bathroom door — her bedroom door again — and yet again — and, finally, the screen door — all in that order. Matthew had kept track and counted. Seven bangs. Then eight. Miss Rose had slammed the screen door twice, coming onto the porch with her paper. Matthew's mouth had been open. *DON'T SPEAK!* Miss Rose had roared at him. He hadn't said a word.

Then Mi had had to bite her cheeks and look away to keep from laughing. Matthew had gone and sat on the steps — as far away from Miss Rose as he could get.

Now, this evening, still in uniform, Miss Rose was seated in her rocker — hers by decree — snapping the paper open so decisively it gave a gunlike noise that sent the chickens scurrying off as if they were about to be slaughtered.

Hunter raised his head.

Nothing.

He laid it back down.

On the far side of the drive, Alex Ross and Alvin Speaks were playing horseshoes.

"Do you have to?" said Miss Rose.

Yes.

They ignored her.

Matthew slid forward, his shoulders hunched and his head halfway down the back of the chair.

Where is Dad?

Where is Ivan Henderson?

"Why don't you write to Rupert?"

"I don't know where he is."

Mi was knitting Matthew's birthday sweater. *Do it now — then it's done*.

"Yes you do," she said.

"No, I don't."

"Of course you do. It begins with *B*."

"Boston."

Matthew crossed his ankles.

Alvin scored a ringer.

"No. Not Boston. Try again."

This was their new game — to see if Matthew could duck his mother's questions. He was a spy. She had caught him. *Don't answer anything. Lie.* What he had to do was throw out everywhere he could think of that began — this time, with *B* — until she trapped him into telling the truth.

Miss Rose rattled her pages.

Matthew said: "Belgium."

"How can Rupert be in Belgium. It's occupied."

"Britain."

"No. I don't think so."

"Why not?"

"You said he was afraid of ships."

"He flew."

"What in?"

"A Lancaster."

"What's that?"

"A new bomber." That was Miss Rose.

Mi and Matthew looked at her. She was still behind the *Evening Star*.

Mi said: "all right. We know he's not in Boston — not in Belgium — and definitely not in Britain."

"Why not in Britain? I told you — he flew there in a Lancaster."

"Rupert in a bomber? *Please.*" Mi laughed. "Try again."

"Bermuda."

"Middle of the Atlantic Ocean. Ships again. 'Fraid not. Give me another."

Matthew was running out of *B*'s — hoarding only the true answer — and that, he must not give up, or he would lose the game. And his honour as a spy.

"Come on," said Mi. "There's lots more *B*'s."

"Brazil," said Miss Rose.

"Aha!" said Mi.

Matthew was furious. Miss Rose had spilled the beans.

Now, Mi knew she had him cornered.

"Where in Brazil? It begins with *R*."

Matthew knew only one city in Brazil that began with *R* — and that was precisely where Rupert and his mysterious mother were spending the summer.

"Rio de Janeiro," said Miss Rose.

Oh, for Pete's sake!

Miss Rose closed her paper.

"They say in here it's the hottest summer since 1936," she told them. "Also that Cary Grant has married Betty Hutton."

"Barbara Hutton," said Mi.

"The Woolworth heiress?"

"That's right. He married her two weeks ago."

"How do you know all this? You haven't even read the paper."

"I told you. I read it two weeks ago."

Miss Rose flashed the paper open, stood up and thrust its pages at Mi. "There. A photograph. Cary Grant and Betty Hutton. *Married*."

"Yes. I see."

There was a indeed a photograph. It showed a smiling Cary Grant and his bride standing on a beach in Hawaii. They were on their honeymoon.

"Barbara," Mi said, and pointed at the caption. "*Barbara*, not *Betty*."

Alvin Speaks delivered another ringer.

"Your game," said Alex Ross. "Good for you!"

Agnes Mortson came to the other side of the screen door and told them supper was on the table.

Nella wafted around the edge of the porch as they were trooping in, and said: "look what I have here. You'll never guess."

She held something trapped in her hands, and when she opened them, it flew away.

It was a butterfly.

Matthew thought: *everything today begins with* B.

Except for Dad. *And* Ivan.

The C.O.'s back was to Graeme. He was looking out the window at the parade ground. *Group Captain Eugene Barker, D.F.C., Commanding Officer.* That's what it said on the door to his office.

Graeme stood at attention, hatless, in front of the desk. He was perspiring. He licked his lips. Salt. His hands, at his sides, were clenched.

"I'm not going to dwell on this, Forbes. I'm just going to tell you."

The C.O. turned.

He sat down.

"You know how much faith I've invested in you. You know how much I depend on you. These premises — this station could not function without you."

"Sir."

"You are in grave danger, Forbes. Extremely grave. I trust you know why."

"Sir."

"I put my reputation on the line for you the last time you got into trouble. Everyone said I was crazy. But I believed — and I still do — that you were the right man for the job — and I believed you deserved the right to prove yourself."

"Sir."

"And — to a large degree — you have."

"Thank you, sir."

The C.O. pushed some papers around on top of his desk. He stroked his moustache with his fingers and picked up a pen and put it down. He was tired. He wanted to be doing anything but this — saying anything else but what had to be said. Surely he didn't have to go into details. Forbes knew what he'd been doing. The drinking. That woman. And ...

He looked at his wife and children in their frame.

"On the twelfth of August ..." he said.

... you will be replaced as Adjutant by Squadron-Leader ...

"... we are to play host to the Prime Minister."

"Sir."

"He is to pay an official visit here on the occasion of the arrival of Squadron-Leader Red Wilson. You've heard of him, of course."

"Red" Wilson, D.F.C. and Bar — hero of the Battle of Britain.

"Yes, sir."

"Squadron-Leader Wilson is to tour the country, Halifax to Vancouver. In a Spitfire, Forbes. Exciting. Yes?"

"Yes, sir. Very."

"The whole affair involves a major War Bond drive. Get out all the big guns. The Spitfire. Wilson — and, of course, the initial event to take place here because of the British Commonwealth Air Training Plan — of which we are the centre."

"Sir."

"And so ..."

You're gone, Forbes. Drunken. Irresponsible. Undependable ...

"I'm expecting you to bring yourself back into line accordingly."

Graeme blinked.

"Understood?"

"Yes, sir. Understood. And ..."

"Yes?"

"And thank you, sir."

"Don't thank me, Forbes. We aren't there yet. Just remember — I'm watching."

"Yes, sir."

Barker picked up the sheets of paper in front of him, shuffled them and tapped them into form. "There's a promotion in this, if you stick it out. Your last chance to gain the rank your administrative skills deserve."

Squadron Leader Forbes.

"Otherwise ..."

"Sir?"

"Otherwise, I will have no choice but to let you go. You will be posted — possibly for the last time — and I assure you, it will not be pleasant."

"Sir."

Barker looked at Graeme with a manufactured steely glare. When he spoke, it might have been a death sentence. "Saskatchewan, Forbes. Town named Dafoe. Temperatures of fifty below." He paused. "Shack-town. And dry. Only females: loyal wives, school-age girls and dogs."

"Yes, sir."

Silence.

"You may go, now."

"Sir."

The C.O. waved him off.

Graeme departed.

Barker closed his eyes. *Thank God. Dinnertime. Mary. The children. Day's end.*

He opened his eyes and stood up. Beyond his family in their frame, there was a second photograph. His sloop — *The Swallow.*
He sighed.
I wish I'd joined the Navy.

At table, Matthew sat beside Mi, across from Nella Mott. Nella had Alvin on her right and Alex on her left. Miss Rose played *father* and sat at the head of the table. On Matthew's left, an empty chair informed them all that — yet again — Mrs Delaney would be taking supper in her room.

"She's poorly," said Agnes — setting sweating pitchers of ice-cold milk and water on the cloth.

"She's never anything else," said Miss Rose.

"It's the heat, much as anything," said Agnes. "Who can blame her? All them dreaded operations — all them pills — all them 'strictions on her intake. Not a lick o' salt. It would drive me crazy!"

"She's overweight," said Miss Rose. "Pass the 'tato salad."

Miss Rose had now lived so long at The Willows, she had fallen victim to some of Agnes Mortson's unique variations on the English language. *'Tato salad* made up part of the staple Willows' diet, along with *devilish eggs* and *'mato saniches.* Reference had been made to *seizure salad,* but one had not yet appeared at table. Mi had no difficulty in working out what all these menu items were — but one night, when Agnes announced they would be eating *hide off the hog,* the look on Matthew's face was too much and Mi had to leave the table on the excuse that she needed the washroom. Later, Nella said: *you haven't heard anything yet. Just wait until something makes her* flustrated!

The Mortsons never ate with the guests, except when Henry had his breakfast with the two Hydro workers. His hours were so entirely different from the others' that he took his meals in the kitchen, according to his schedule. Agnes always ate with him, feeling it was her wifely duty to do so, and her duty as hostess and landlady to remain available to the guests at mealtime. She maintained a sort of station at the foot of the table, opposite Miss Rose, where she would oversee the ebb and flow of each meal's progress.

Truth be told, Mi wrote to Eloise, *Agnes Mortson is one of the best cooks in the whole wide world — bar none.*

And the rest of the people are heaven.

The young man, Speaks, never utters. Presumably, he has a voice — though we never hear it. He has already been in the war and come back. Wounded. No one knows where, or how. He shows no marks and his friend — an older man who lives with him down the hall — never mentions any, though he must, one assumes, see him naked going to bed and getting up. I find them very touching, this pair. The older man, whose name is Alex Ross, must be approaching fifty and Speaks can't be any more than twenty-five or so. When you see them together, all the myths about men lacking tenderness are completely dispelled. Though both of them are hard as nails in every other way — physically and in terms of their work — they exude a kind of quiet affection for everything around them — grass and trees — the cows. Even for their knives and forks and the tablecloth!

As for Miss Rose, there's something there that I can't determine. She has the manner and appearance of the Nurse from Hell — but I'm certain there must be more to her than that. She has a round flat face and round flat spectacles and the grimmest mouth I've ever seen. She pulls her hair so tight to the back of her neck, I swear it must be some sort of private torture she inflicts on herself — like those monks who beat themselves with whips. And her body, also — bound in with corsets — positively tubular — tied up in white. And yet, when the glasses come off, her eyes tell a different story — eyes like an animal suffering in silence. Know what I mean? Like a dog with cancer.

Graeme? What can I tell you? He's with that woman and he's drinking. And yet, by some miracle, he's at his desk every morning and performs his duties, so I'm told, quite well. Neither perfect nor dreadful, in terms of compe- tence — in terms of demeanour. Certainly not God's gift — but not the devil's, either, the way he used to be. Is this what people mean by mellow? *Maybe not. Graeme, I doubt, will ever mellow. Too much smouldering going on. So far, we see him only on Sundays. Otherwise, so he says, he's always on duty. (!)*

Have you met his room-mate, Ivan? I can't remember. Nice man. Rides a motorcycle. Matthew is in love with him. The way boys always are with dashing heroes.

Have seen Roy twice. Perhaps he's told you. I hope he told you I'm looking well — because I am. In fact, Mister Louis B. Mayer — who is up here scouting for new movie stars — tells me I could be the next Joan Crawford. Or was it Joan Fontaine? Or am I entirely mistaken, and was it Garbo, Ingrid Bergman ... Olivia de Havilland?

Watch out. I'm on the warpath!

We survive.

Love to the dreadful Mum — more than love to you.

Michael.

Mi set her pen down.

I thought you were going to tell her about Ivan.

I can't. Not in writing. It wouldn't be proper.

Liar.

Please ...

You're afraid that if you start to put him on paper, you'll find out you're in love with him.

I am not in love with him!

She stood up.

Sounds familiar ...

Mi lighted a cigarette. It was midnight.

Sounds like the lady doth protest too much.

I am not in love with him. Not. It's just ...

What? Just what?

I'm losing Gray. I'm losing him. And ...

Unh-hunh.

I'm losing my will to save him. To win him back. He's becoming like the villain in a story — all one colour.

Grey.

Very funny. The least you could be is serious. He's *gone.* Gone — left — departed. Out there somewhere, flailing at his demons and I'm tired of it. Tired of it. Exhausted ...

There's one more word here, Michael.

Yes. I know.

What is it? Say it.

Beaten.

Go to bed.

Yes. Tired. I'm tired.

Mi undressed and put on her nightie. No moon tonight. Not yet.

She folded the letter to Eloise, turned out the light on the bureau and stubbed her cigarette.

You haven't brushed your hair.

To hell with it.

Or your teeth.

To hell with them.

Shouldn't you pee?

No.

Yes. Go and pee. Then you won't have to get up at four A.M.

Mi went over to the door, opened it and looked into the hall. No one.

Nella's light was out. Mi moved along the hall barefooted.

She used, but did not flush, the toilet. This was the house rule, kindness of Miss Rose. No one was to flush the toilet after midnight, for fear of waking her up. *My work, you know. My people depend on me for their lives.*

Matthew's door was ajar.

Mi went in.

She stood by the bureau, listening to him breathe.

I love you, Mattie.

His window was open.

From the fields, she heard a cow-bell, followed by some lowing. Distress. *I'm lost.*

Aren't we all.

Blowing Matthew a kiss, she left his door ajar, as he might have intended, and went along the hall to her room.

Sitting on the edge of her bed, she imagined all the people sleeping and dreaming. Alvin's nightmares crouching on the windowsill and the dreams of Alex on the floor beneath the bed.

Next door, the Mortsons no doubt slept like effigies — with pots and pans and pitchforks floating in the air above them. Agnes and Henry, their hands at peace, folded benignly on their breasts — smiling, contented — with morning already upon them in their dreams.

As for Miss Rose, her body — freed of its impediments — would lie becalmed as a lake whose shores were the parameters of her sagging mattress and whose islands were her breasts and, at the foot, an archipelago of toes. She would dream of sounds as white and soft as unstarched cotton, while a silent river of ether carried off her patients, one by one.

Nella sat up to sleep, with seven pillows to support her. *The Seven Pillows of Wisdom*, she had called them — smiling her smile and clasping her knees. She had explained that, lying flat, she would cease to breathe. *It is called* apnoea, she told Mi — *a word, for all its dangers, I find rather beautiful.* In her dreams, she sat in leafy trees, unseen, while she counted over all the names of everything that lived. *My name,* she would say in the dreams, *is legion.*

Mi lay back and held the sheet between her breasts.

Matthew is alive down the hall. Sleeps on his side — arms raised — legs splayed — an all-out spread of boy. By dawn, the pillows will be on the floor — and the sheets around his ankles. He will dream tonight ...

... of drowning. And of rising to the surface with a shout — *The City of St Andrew's* far below him — Rupert rafting to Rio — and Ivan waiting on the shore.

And my dreams? Mine?

She turned to one side and closed her eyes. With three deep breaths, though unaware of it, she began to drift.

Heroes and villains. One and the other. All Graeme's longing to be a hero dashed on the rocks of his large ambition to slink out of sight — cut the painter and float away on a sea of booze and blondes.

No use trying to hail him from the strand. Only heroes have ears. Villains are deaf. They turn their backs on distress and train their sights on the farthest shore.

Almost all the way to sleep. A distant voice began to sing.

> *My Bonnie lies over the ocean;*
> *My Bonnie lies over the sea.*
> *My Bonnie lies over the ocean —*
> *Oh, bring back my Bonnie to me.*

Far, far away, there was a sound. A hive of bees had been loosed. A swarm of hornets. A cloud of wasps.

A motorcycle. That was it.

Mi slept.

7th August, 1942

Matthew was in *The Bluebell* with Nella. He had rowed them through the marsh and into the Bay. Hot and still, as every day seemed to be, it was even hotter along the shore because of the sun reflecting off the water. Faraway on the horizon, a flotilla of tall white clouds was assembling. Nella said they were the Spanish Armada and probably contained hailstones.

"You see how they boil up over the top? That's a sure sign we may be going to have a storm."

"Do you want to go farther out?" said Matthew.

"Not necessarily. We could land here and search for stones, if you like."

"Okay."

Matthew began to manoeuvre *The Bluebell* back towards the shore.

"Funny, how when there's going to be a storm all the cows lie down," said Nella.

Matthew looked over his shoulder. Beyond the beach, the land rolled up into Henry Mortson's tall-grass meadows — and nineteen languid cows were lying there watching Matthew's every move like an audience. The bull was standing off to one side, as much as to say: *stuff and nonsense, all these rumours of rain. Get up at once!* But his cows paid no attention.

"They're all facing in the same direction," said Matthew.

"That's right. They face the storm."

Matthew felt the soft crush of sand beneath the keel and the crunch of pebbles. Shipping the oars, he stood up and climbed over the gunwales into the shallows.

"Warm," he said.

"How lovely," said Nella. "I shall take off my shoes."

Doing so, she joined Matthew in the water, slipping her plimsolls into her work-basket and her umbrella under her arm.

"Delicious!"

Nella waded onto the dry stones and deposited her things while Matthew beached *The Bluebell*.

"Oh, what a heavenly day!" Nella said, hurrying back into the Bay. Lifting her skirts, she walked out far enough to have the water cover her knees. Closing her eyes, she tilted her head until the brim of her summertime hat was brushing against her shoulder blades. "What have we done to deserve such wonders?" she said. "What can we have done, that God is so kind to us?"

Matthew could not answer this and said nothing.

Nella opened her eyes.

"If you look up there, you'll see ten million herring gulls floating on the updraft. See there? Millions of them." Something of an exaggeration. "Millions ..." Her voice drifted off and Matthew swore she was counting.

Walking out to stand beside her, he shaded his eyes and looked up.

At first, he saw nothing — only the sky — and said so.

Nella said: "you have to close your eyes first."

He did so.

"Wait," said Nella.

Matthew was afraid of losing his balance, and nearly did.

"Now," said Nella.

He opened his eyes. And there they were — impossibly high — ghost shapes, almost — sailing in circles, higher and higher. *Millions* of them — wide and white and rising.

"The stars have sprouted wings," said Nella.

Herring gulls.

Matthew thought of the wings on Ivan's jacket. *An eagle's wings.*

He shaded his eyes. The cuffs of his shorts were wet. In spite of that, he could have stood there forever. And, evidently, the same was true of Nella. He looked at her — curious. *She might be Rupert's sister.* That was it. She was Rupert through and through, with her eye on everything that moved. The only difference was, no one ever came in a big black car to drive her away. Her adventures were confined to here — *this place and all its wonders.* For Nella Mott, here was the whole wide world.

"I am going to sit in the meadow," she said — and turned. "You may bring whatever stones you find and we can drink the ginger beer I've brought."

She was wading past him.

"The sun," she said — as though it was all that need be said. "The sun," and she gave it a wave.

Hot.

On the shore, she collected her things and sat with them at the edge of the field on a wide flat stone. Her legs and feet were gleaming. "We are alive," she whispered — and raised her umbrella.

Mi and Ivan were walking on the driveway. The Harley was parked beneath the willows. Ivan wore his leather pants and jacket, having come to take Matthew for his motorcycle ride.

In the meantime, they avoided Agnes in her kitchen and Mrs Delaney in her bedroom by walking to the gate and back — and back to the gate again. It was four o'clock.

"I wish we could go to your room," said Ivan.

"So do I," said Mi.

But she was glad they couldn't. She felt endangered by his presence — or would, if they climbed the stairs.

"Do you know," she said, "I don't know anything about you. Not even where you were born."

"I was born and grew up in Regina."

"A westerner."

"Sa — skat — chew — an," he said. "Where I fell in love."

Oh.

He looked at her and smiled. "With the sky."

Mi turned away. She had no right to be relieved, but she was.

"I've never been," she said. "I'd love to see it. The sky. The prairie. All that distance ..."

"Yes."

"... in all directions."

"Yes."

"But you left."

"Yes."

"In spite of loving it? Was it the war? Did you leave because of the war?"

"No."

Mi stopped and looked at him.

"No?"

"No. I left because of my father."

They walked on.

"That sounds ... interesting. Do you mean he forced you to leave?"

"No. It was because he died."

"Oh."

"Finally."

"I'm sorry?"

"I left because he *finally* died."

"You obviously didn't care for him."

"Not at the end. No. He was an alcoholic."

Graeme.

"He'd driven my mother away when I was a kid. Broke her and drove her off."

Me.

"I never really knew my mother," Ivan said. "I barely remember what she looked like. There weren't any photographs. He destroyed them all. Tore them to pieces and flushed them down the toilet. He brought me up, if you can call it that, all by himself."

"All by himself."

"Yes. It was his weapon. His blackmail. He held it over my head for the rest of his life. *You owe me,* he would say. *You owe me everything.*"

Mi touched his arm — its leather cool and sensual. "I'm sorry," she said. "What a grim, bloody way to grow up."

"Yes. But you grow up fast." Ivan looked away at the trees. "For his last three years, I was all he had. And, basically, he was all *I* had. I became his parent — his mother and his father. He used to fall asleep on the floor and mess himself. He'd cry, because he was afraid. He set himself on fire, once. Smoking."

"A nightmare ..."

"Yes. A nightmare. Then he died. In his sleep, thank God. In the end, at least, some mercy."

Mi and Ivan leaned on the gate.

Mi ran her finger down the long, extended zipper of Ivan's jacket.

"Oh ..." she said. But that was all.

"Yes," said Ivan.

Mi looked away. "Damn," she said. "They're coming back from the river."

"What do I hold onto?" said Matthew.

"Me," Ivan told him. "Put your arms under my arms like this." He demonstrated. "You won't fall. I promise."

"Who gets on first?"

"I do." Ivan mounted the motorcycle and pulled on a pair of black leather gloves. "Okay," he said. "All aboard!"

Matthew raised his right leg, the way Ivan had done — but he had to hop on the other foot to get all the way over.

Ivan put on a pair of goggles and booted the kick-stand. He kept the bike upright with his left foot on the ground while he turned the key and started the engine.

"Here we go!" he shouted — and just as they passed through the gate: "heigh-ho, Silver! Away!"

The gravel sideroad threw up such a cloud of dust, Mi could barely see them as they rode off.

Matthew wished he had tied a bandanna across his mouth, the way that cowboys did. He closed his eyes.

Ivan sat up straight in front of him, elbows spread, hands palm down on the throttle and the brake. He wore no hat and the collar of his leather jacket had no wings and looked like something worn by a dog.

Matthew held tightly at first but when they came to the highway, he let go.

"What you have to do," said Ivan, "is lean around the corners. When I lean, you lean. Understand?"

"Yes."

"You okay back there?"

"Yes."

"Here we go, then."

Again, the engine leapt into gear and Matthew put his arms under Ivan's arms and leaned when Ivan leaned — all the way over — this way — that way — and in between, lying forward now with his cheek against Ivan's leather back.

It's just the same as learning how to skate, he thought. *Lean in, lean out, lean forward ...*

The Harley began to pick up serious speed and soon they were going so fast that he could barely think consecutive thoughts. The noise of it was wonderful — loud and all the noise there was: part the engine, part the wind, part the skimming voice of the road beneath the wheels.

Matthew closed his eyes and watched the flickering light through his lids as trees flew by, and fences, houses, barns and open fields. The smell of the jacket beneath his cheek had become the smell of Ivan himself — of leather, oil and gasoline — and the feel of him was solid, warm and dry. *And what? I don't know. Alive.* Pushing back at him. Huge. Massive. Enormous.

Matthew held one hand with the other, fingers locked and pressed into fists beneath his thumbs.

It darkened.

Night?

How can it be?

He opened his eyes.

The sky had been eclipsed.

Matthew felt he would never speak again.

The storm had come.

Ivan pulled to a momentary stop. "We'd best go back," he said, "before all hell breaks loose."

Matthew said nothing. Nothing.

They moved out onto the road. Ivan made a wide U-turn. There was not another vehicle in sight.

"I'll get us there in a minute flat." Ivan turned and smiled. "You ready for this? It's Spitfire time."

Matthew could only nod.

Ivan gunned the motor. A deathly calm had settled over the landscape, while above it, Nella Mott's Spanish Armada was piling higher and higher — white no longer, but copper-green — the colour of the lamps at home. And brass, the colour of lightning drawn with crayons.

"The sky is green!" he shouted — but Ivan could not hear him. "Green!" Matthew shouted. He'd never seen anything like it. *What kind of storm is this?*

There was a rumbling noise beneath the noise of the Harley — a wide, dark roaring sound. Matthew clung to Ivan's back.

It began to rain.

He locked his hands again into fists. He was afraid — and not afraid. It was odd. The fear was steadied — level. It had no peaks — it was simply there, a kind of fear Matthew had never experienced before. He began to press the whole of his body into Ivan's back — his bare knees pushed up hard against the undersides of Ivan's thighs. The fear made a lump in his stomach — a ball in his diaphragm — weights with shapes that were somehow comforting.

The dark beyond his eyelids was now almost the dark of night and the rain beat down like bullets onto the top of his head, his shoulders and the side of his face that was exposed. It was cold, the rain. Freezing cold and it stung. He licked his lips. It tasted like melted icicles.

Matthew felt a second leap in speed. Ivan's body straightened and pushed back even harder against him. In seconds, so it seemed, they came to The Willows sideroad.

Lean.

Lean.

They turned.

The smell of wet gravel, sand, meadows and wire fences flooded in around them.

Matthew felt a sudden, new and curious sensation — unidentified — unaccountable — in the dip beneath his groin — between his legs. Spreading up towards his heart and down towards his knees.

Something's going to happen.

Something's going to happen.

Then it did.

The Harley bumped over the stones that signalled the turn into The Willows' drive. Matthew's groin began to flood.

Why?

What?

Wet. Wet.

He opened his eyes.

Very slowly, he pulled away from Ivan's leather.

He could barely breathe.

Mi was standing on the porch. All the chickens had come up off the lawn and were roosting on the rocking chairs. Ivan made a second turn that delivered Matthew to the steps.

"You look more like two drowned sailors than motorcycle riders," Mi said. "Come on in and get dried off."

Matthew hesitated. He would have preferred to be wet all over. A precaution, in case his mother could see what had happened to him. He dared not look, himself. *There might be blood down there — or something. I don't know what.*

Ivan was still seated on the bike.

"Can you stay to supper?" Mi asked.

There was a flash of lightning — followed almost at once by thunder. The chickens flapped their wings and then resettled.

"Thanks," said Ivan, lifting his goggles. "But I can't. I've got to get back. I have a date in the mess."

Mi winced, but turned it into a smile.

"A date, eh?"

"Yes." Ivan was grinning.

"Anyone we know?" said Mi.

"It's possible. Name of Forbes."

"You've got a date with Graeme? Well, well, well. I should have thought you'd seen enough of him — day in, day out, the way you do."

"No. We never get tired of each other."

Liar.

Lightning.

Thunder.

"Shall I tell him you'll be there on Sunday for the buffet?"

No — god-damn it.

"Yes." And then: "yes," again. And finally: "give him our love."

"Will do."

Ivan took out a handkerchief and wiped the rain from his face and goggles.

"You sure you don't want to come in?"

"Would if I could — but I can't. Adios."

"No. Wait!"

This was Matthew.

"You haven't told me how fast we went."

"Any guesses?"

"A hundred? A hundred and fifty? More."

Ivan smiled and reached into his pocket. Mi watched.

"See this?"

It was a silver dollar.

Matthew nodded.

"See the old king?" Ivan said. "George V. That's how long I've had it. 1934."

"What's it got to do with how fast we went?"

Ivan winked at Mi.

"How many pennies in here?" he asked — and flashed the dollar.

"A hundred."

"Well, then," said Ivan. "Now you know how fast we went. One whole silver dollar's worth."

One hundred miles an hour.

Ivan pulled down his goggles and gunned the motor.

"See you!"

And was gone.

8th August, 1942

On Saturday, Mi drove to town with Henry and shopped for notepaper and envelopes. Blue. She also bought a bottle of Scotch, a bottle of wine and two packs of Guinea Gold cigarettes.

On her way back to the truck, she paused in the shadow of a toy store.

Something for Matthew.

She looked in the window.

Yes.

Inside, she bought the miniature version of a Spitfire in a small green box.

On the sidewalk, having left, she turned around and went back in.

"Have you another?" she said.

"Yes, ma'am. They're all the rage."

"So I understand. May I have one more, please."

"Certainly."

"And would you wrap it — could you wrap it as a gift?"

9th August, 1942

Sunday was hot and languid. Friday's rain had all been turned to steam.

Mi wore her simplest dress. Not blue, but white. *Your virgin's dress*, Eloise had said. She also wore the blue-and-white shoes and tied Nella's scarf around her neck. It was becoming her trademark in the mess.

Matthew wore long trousers. Not the ducks, but others. Bought in June, they had lain unused in the middle drawer of his bureau with the promise, every day, that he would wear them *tomorrow*.

They were khaki, with cuffs.

He carried the Spitfire in his pocket.

In the parade ground, standing at the bottom step, Mi said: "may I take your arm, kind sir?"

"Yes'm."

Matthew crooked his elbow.

"You look terrific in those trousers," Mi said.

Matthew blushed. "Thanks."

"You're supposed to return the compliment."

"Oh. Uhm ..."

"How about: *you look terrific, too, Mum*?"

"You look terrific, too, Mum."

"Thank you. Lead on."

They moved up the steps, past the doors, down the corridor into the anteroom, past all the hats on the table and into the mess itself.

There were the white-clothed trestles of food. There were the chairs and sofas. There were the lamps and magazines. And there were all the people. Men and women. Mostly women.

Someone was playing the piano.

"It's Dad."

"Yes."

And someone was sitting beside him.

"Who's that?"

Mi paused only long enough to clear her throat.

"A friend of your father's," she said. "Her name is Sue Anne Howard."

Roy was standing by the bar, watching.

Mi turned to Matthew. "Why don't you go and find Ivan, hon?"

Matthew said: "he doesn't like the buffet."

"Well, you could look. Last thing he said to me was *see you Sunday.*"

"Okay."

Matthew hesitated. He looked at Graeme and Sue Anne Howard — and put his hands in his pockets. Mi watched this and touched his chin, turning his face towards her. She smiled.

"All is well," she said. "I'll be fine."

"Really?"

"Yes. I'm going to go and say hello to Uncle Roy."

"Okay."

"Don't have more than twenty glasses of lemonade."

Matthew grinned. "No, ma'am," he said, and walked away.

Mi waved at Roy.

Crossing the room, she was aware of being watched from several quarters. *There goes the Adjutant's wife*, they would be saying. Women would say it with a secret smile. Men would say it with an edge of warning. *Let them.*

Graeme was playing "These Foolish Things" — an unfortunate but interesting choice, since he knew it was one of Mi's favourites.

"Hello, Roy."

"Mi."

"What's that you're drinking?"

"Rye and ginger ale."

"I'll have the same."

Roy turned to the barman and Mi kept her back to Graeme. And Sue Anne.

Mustn't forget Sue Anne.

Not likely.

Hot, isn't it.

Go away.

Now, now — mustn't lose our temper.

Roy handed her the drink and said: "you want to stand here — or what?"

"I think I'd prefer to *what*," said Mi.

Roy chuckled. "Good for you."

"It feels like a scene in a movie. As if they're all expecting me to take a gun out of my bag and shoot him. Cheers."

They drank.

"You want to go out on the terrace?"

"No. Thanks. I'm trying to get up the nerve to speak to him."

"Is that wise?"

"Of course it is. I can't be here and not *know*, for heaven's sake. Everybody else knows — why not me."

"What had you thought of saying?"

"*Hello*."

Roy shook his head and chuckled again. "You could give lessons," he said.

"I've met her, you know. He doesn't know it — but I have. Two weeks ago, out there on the terrace. Come to think of it, *she* doesn't know."

"How come?"

"We did not exchange names." Mi laughed. "Good grief — I sound just like Greer Garson!"

Graeme broke into "Waltzing Matilda."

Mi turned and looked at him.

He seemed to be enjoying himself — oblivious of his surroundings. He was alone with Sue Anne. Perhaps at sea on the *Île de France* — or in New Orleans or maybe a low-down New York dive. Their lives were turning into the lyrics of a song and the stuff of magazine fiction. *Michael stood at the bar and watched her husband through a cloud of smoke ...*

She took out her cigarettes, turning her handbag so that Roy wouldn't see Ivan's Spitfire, wrapped in its glossy paper and tied with green ribbon.

"What's the news from Eloise?" she asked.

"Good," Roy said. "She's going to be here on Tuesday."

"Oh — how wonderful. Wonderful. Perfect. Heaven."

"She wants to see the Spitfire ceremony and the P.M. To say nothing of *Red* Wilson. Red hair, you know — like her husband. And I was able to get special dispensation through my friend Graeme Forbes." Roy smiled. "Happens to be the Adjutant."

"Yes. I've heard of him."

"El was wondering if ... Don't worry if it isn't possible, but she said you'd said there might be room at The Willows."

Mi's mind went blank.

The Willows. Eloise.

Ivan.

"No."

Roy looked startled.

"It's just that — they're full — and ... I had thought she could sleep with me, but ..."

"Not a good time for visitors?"

What does he know?

"No. All this ... you can guess how I feel. I feel ..."

"It's okay."

"No. It's not okay. Not if I promised. But — I hardly sleep at all. I'd drive her crazy."

"Sure. I'll book a room at The Green Parrot."

"Will you be able to stay with her?"

"No. Unfortunately. I'm required here. Until it's over. All leave cancelled."

"Well — we can certainly see each other. Lunch and everything. I haven't seen her since June ..." Mi faltered. She glanced at Graeme and away again. "Oh, God, Roy. What am I going to do?"

"Play it through. It's bound to end. She'll get tired of him. Go away. That's how it always ends, with Graeme. *Love 'em and leave 'em.* You know that."

"Have you — met her?" Mi asked.

"Unh-hunh."

"I'll tell you the truth. I rather liked her. Sweet. Endearing."

"And pretty." Roy smiled.

"Passable."

"Are you sure you want to stay?"

"Yes."

"Can I help?"

"Maybe. Perhaps you would walk me over to the piano."

"Now?"

"Not if you don't want to."

"No. I think it's probably a good idea. How's your drink holding up?"

"I'd better have another. Thanks."

Graeme had stopped playing. Sue Anne was picking out one-fingered tunes. *Michael took a deep breath and faced the piano. Every eye in the room was on her. She opened her pocketbook and looked inside. There it was ... the derringer.*

Rooty-toot-toot — three times she shoot, right through that bar-room door ...

"There you go, then."

"Thanks."

Mi accepted the drink and stubbed her cigarette in the ashtray on the bar.

"I feel as if I've just been asked to take all my clothes off and walk down Yonge Street."

"I'm right beside you."

"Yes. But you're fully clothed."

"Shall we go?"

"Yes."

They started towards the piano. Sue Anne's back was nearest. She was laughing. Giggling.

When Mi and Roy were about to close the gap between them, Sue Anne stood up.

"You want another?" she said.

Graeme nodded. He was lighting a cigarette.

Sue Anne turned. She had an empty glass in either hand.

"Oh."

"Hello," said Mi.

"It's you."

"Yes. Me."

"I wondered when we'd meet again," Sue Anne said. "You were so kind to me that night." She turned to Roy. "Hello."

"Hello."

Sue Anne turned back to Graeme. He was *noodling*. Chords. No melody.

Sue Anne said to Mi: "I told you, didn't I, that I'd met someone?"

"Yes. You told me."

"Well, this is him. Mister Maestro!" She was beaming — still the child. "Graeme?" Graeme turned. "This is the lady I told you about ... the one who was so nice."

Graeme started to rise.

Mi said: "don't get up." And then: "hello, Graeme."

Sue Anne was suitably bewildered. "You know each other?"

"Yes. I'm his wife."

Roy put out his hand. Sue Anne folded like a sawdust doll, her arms against her stomach. Still bent double, she said to Graeme — barely audible: "you told me she wasn't coming. You said she wouldn't be here." She straightened. All her colour was gone. "You *promised*. You said I'd never have to meet her."

Mi took her arm.

Sue Anne raised her head and said: "oh, God — I'm so sorry."

Mi said nothing.

Sue Anne, still clutching the empty glasses, looked at Graeme and said: "you bastard." Only Mi heard her. Then Sue Anne turned, dropped the empty glasses on the floor — and left.

In the silence that followed, several people looked away. Slowly, the trio by the piano were isolated. The chatter recommenced.

People drifted off. Nothing had happened. Some glass had broken. A woman had left the room — that was all.

Graeme said: "you might have handled that differently."

"So might you," said Mi. "But it's done."

Graeme stood up. He said nothing. He went to the bar.

Mi waited.

Roy sat down.

Graeme did not return. He stayed, standing at the bar with his back to the room.

Mi said: "thank you," to Roy and crossed the room and stood beside Graeme.

"This doesn't need to be a scene," she said. "It's not an argument. I did what I thought should be done — and I'm not going to apologize for it."

Graeme stared at the smoke from his cigarette.

"In time," Mi said, "we might have met under worse circumstances than these ..." *I could have found you in bed with her.* "Please. Will you come outside. I can't say all this here."

"All what?"

"Everything. Everything there is to say — which isn't much. After all, how can it be, when so little has happened that hasn't all happened before. There's barely anything new to say. Except ..."

"Yes?"

"Please. Come outside."

She started away towards the terrace. Slowly, Graeme followed.

Mi went all the way to the far end, and waited without turning. When he finally stood beside her, she looked right at him.

"I have never, in all our married life, thought once of leaving you. *Not once.* In spite of ... everything."

Graeme lifted one foot and rested it on the lower railing, leaning

forward with his arms on the top. They might have been dis-
cussing the view.

Mi said: "now — the thought of leaving you is ever present,
Graeme. Ever present." She leaned back, pushing hard against the
rail. "Good God," she said. "I don't even call you *Gray* any more."

"Does this mean you *are* going to leave?"

Mi took a deep breath — and waited.

"No," she said.

At last, he looked at her.

She went on: "we have a son. Remember? Name of Matthew.
And, god-damn it, Graeme — he needs a father. He needs a father.
Right now. *Now.* He needs — he requires — HE MUST HAVE
— the services of a father. You."

Graeme said nothing.

Mi said: "I've given up expecting to have a husband. But I will
not deprive him of his father. Me? I can't fight for me any more.
But for him I can — and for him, I will. And I will not deprive you
of the privilege — I will not allow you to just ... heave a sigh and
walk away."

She waited.

Graeme was silent. He drank.

Mi said: "furthermore — he needs *us.* Jesus Christ, Graeme — we
both lost our parents. Your father died and your god-damned mother
went into permanent mourning. Gone. My parents divorced. And
believe you me, that is loss. With a capital *L.* So — in answer to your
question: *will I leave you?* I repeat ... I reiterate. *No.*"

Mi stood up straight and looked back at the crowded mess.
There was music again — and laughter. "I'm going inside," she
said. "And I'm going to send Matthew out here — alone. He may
have something to tell you — he may not. But you should know,

just in case it slips your mind, he is not a little boy any more."
Unlike his father. "He could use some male companionship.
WHICH I CANNOT PROVIDE!"

Graeme still said nothing.

"All right?"

He nodded.

"Maybe we could actually sit together while we eat. You can
bring us up to date on what's going to happen Wednesday, when
the Spitfire arrives. Et cetera ..."

Nothing.

"Graeme — please turn around and look at me."

He paused, lifted his arm away from the rail, and turned.

"I actually do love you," said Mi. "Not you — but the memory
of you. That's what I have. And that's what I'm holding onto —
for the time being. Do you understand?"

Graeme nodded.

Mi said: "I'll send him out, now."

Then she went back inside, while Graeme looked at the sky, as
if there might be a message there, telling him what to do.

Matthew stood in the doorway.

Graeme was watching the Bay.

Far, far away an aeroplane was approaching.

Two other people had come out onto the terrace — a man and
a woman, somewhat older than Mi and Graeme — but they were
standing off to one side looking towards the dipping sun, as Sue
Anne had done.

Matthew thought: *Dad looks tired.*

The woman laughed.

Matthew walked farther out — waited, and then went all the way to the end.

"Hi."

Graeme looked at him and straightened.

"Hi."

"It's nearly time to eat, I guess."

"Yes. You hungry?"

"Maybe. Sure."

"So ..." Graeme smiled. "What's new?"

"I went on the motorcycle with Ivan."

"Yes. He told me."

Then nothing.

They both looked back towards the Bay.

Matthew took the Spitfire from his pocket and held it out.

"Mum gave me this."

"That's nice."

Nothing. Matthew put the aeroplane back in his pocket.

"Dad?"

"Unh-hunh?"

"Are you going to come and see us ever?"

"How do you mean?"

"At The Willows. Ivan comes — but you don't. Is ... is something wrong?"

"I'm busy. Work."

Liar.

"We could go on the river. There's a rowboat."

"Unh-hunh."

"It was neat, when you came in the Harvard and dive-bombed us on the road."

"You liked that, eh?"

"Yes. Thank you."

"You want to go in? Eat?"

"Maybe not quite yet."

"Okay. You stay and I'll go in and join your mother."

And get another drink.

"Dad?"

Graeme had started away and turned back.

"Yes?" And then: "what?"

"Nothing," said Matthew. The man and the woman were watching him. "Sorry. I forget."

"See you inside."

"Yessir."

Graeme departed.

Matthew glanced at the others. "Good evening," he said. *Don't you know it's rude to stare?*

He turned away.

He put his hand in his pocket — drew out the Spitfire — broke its wings — and threw it over the railing.

Watching it fall, he thought: *it should have been on fire.*

Then he went inside.

After finding Matthew and sending him out to Graeme, Mi had gone looking for Ivan.

He was in the corridor beyond his room.

"I was just leaving," he said.

"So I see."

He was wearing his uniform. Also his flight jacket.

"You going flying?"

"No. On the bike."

"Oh. Well — have a good time."

"I'm sorry. I just can't face being in the mess when he's there and you walk in."

"It's all right. I figured it was something like that."

"Want to walk me to the door?"

"Sure."

They went down the steps to the parade ground. Then they went almost to the centre — and stopped. The space around them seemed enormous — not another soul in sight. Mess time. And the sun descending.

"I brought you something," she said.

She handed Ivan the Spitfire.

"What can this be?"

"Open it."

Ivan pulled the ribbon aside and unwrapped the box.

"Oh, for heaven's sake," he said, as he looked inside. "It's beautiful." He lifted it into the dwindling light. "*Zoom!*"

"Hah!"

"I could kiss you."

"Don't. We're a trifle over-exposed out here."

"Thank you."

"Keep it with you. Always."

"I will."

Ivan put the Spitfire back in its box and the box in his flight-jacket pocket.

"Give me the wrapping paper," said Mi. "And the ribbon."

She folded them into her purse and snapped it shut.

Ivan's back was to the sun, and Mi had to shade her eyes in order to see him — just as she had when she saw him first and didn't know who he was.

"Ride safely," she said.

"I always do."

"Famous last words, my darling. Never, never say that again."

Ivan smiled. "I'd better go."

"Yes."

"See you."

"Yes."

Why are we always saying goodbye? It's all we ever do.

Mi watched him pass beyond the gate. Then she turned around, waiting for the motorcycle engine to start — hearing, however, nothing but her own footsteps. *Left — right. Left — right. Left.*

Me — on parade.

12th August, 1942

The bed was wet. The sheet was on the floor. Mi's nightgown had ridden up almost to her shoulders. She lifted herself onto her elbows and stared at the window.

The moon was setting. The sky had morning in it. The air itself was full of light.

She got up and crossed the room, her nightgown falling to its proper length around her ankles. At the bureau, she got out one of Graeme's pre-war handkerchiefs — kept for their size — and began to dry her breasts and neck and under her arms. She had not perspired like this since the summer of '36 — the year the last great heat wave struck.

She went to the window, where the moonlight was bright enough to show the dial of her watch. Four thirty-five.

Beyond the screens, there was a mist — almost a fog — that was translucent, lit as if from within. In the field nearby, the cattle appeared to float on their way to the river to drink. Their legs could not be seen, but only their heads and bodies, swimming through the light.

An owl spoke.

Mi went back and sat on her bed.

Her marriage was over.

She lighted a cigarette.

Four thirty-eight. A.M.

Matthew had said: *where's Dad?*

Well — now we know. He's nowhere, any more. Went inside himself and died.

216

God-damn it.

And me? I don't know who I am. I lost myself somewhere along the way to here.

To this bed. In this room. In a stranger's house.

In this heat.

In this light.

At four thirty-nine A.M. on the morning of August 12th. A Wednesday. 1942.

Dear one. Dear heart.

Bonnie. Bonnie.

Also the stillborn — unnamed.

And Matthew.

Graeme.

Ivan.

Me.

Mi.

All this wet — and not one tear.

Space. Space. Just space. And emptiness. Nothing. Nothing. War.

"Spitfire day!" said Matthew. "Spitfire day and Red Wilson!"

The fog had not risen. Nor the heat. Beyond the screens, the chickens and the willow trees were ghosts.

Mi and Matthew were standing in the hall. Any minute, Eloise Best would arrive. She had saved enough gasoline coupons to drive all the way from Toronto and had telephoned the night before from The Green Parrot. Tonight, they would all eat there together, to celebrate the arrival of the Spitfire and the Prime Minister. *Mustn't forget the Prime Minister,* Mi had said.

Matthew wore his long trousers. Also, his St Andrew's blazer. Mi wore grey. *It's tasteful — just in case I have to shake the P.M.'s hand. And my highest heels — in case I get to meet Red Wilson. One way or another — every inch the Adjutant's wife, in my small black hat — with veil.*

In the yard, Eloise honked her horn.

Everyone, including Hunter, went out onto the porch. The chickens did not move.

"This fog," Eloise said, getting out of the car, "is absolute hell on wheels. Hello, my darlings."

They embraced — Matthew first, then Mi.

Eloise whistled and told Matthew he'd grown like a giraffe. Which he had — and to such a degree that Mi and Agnes had had to let down the cuffs on his trousers and the sleeves of his shirt and blazer.

Eloise wore a fez and a dark crêpe dress that made her look like someone posing for the cover of a magazine.

"*Très chic*," said Mi.

"*Très* bloody expensive!" said Eloise. "We'd better go. I had to crawl along the road."

They got into the car and shouted goodbye to Agnes and Nella. Hunter started to bark — and no sooner had Eloise turned the engine and released the brake than they instantly disappeared. Everyone.

Hunter could be heard all the way to the gate and almost to the highway. Matthew thought: *the fog is barking*.

The parade ground was packed. Three squadrons of airmen, ground crew and WDs were lined up in flights facing the reviewing stand. Each flight consisted of thirty men or women in three rows of ten. Their backs were to the airfield beyond the road. In the fog, the most distant figures were barely visible.

When the Prime Minister appeared, Matthew thought he was the smallest man he had ever seen. *William Lyon Mackenzie King, never married, had no Queen. Isn't that the strangest thing? William Lyon Mackenzie King ...* They had chanted this at school. It was thought to be the height of disrespect — almost on a par with saying *Jesus Christ* out of chapel.

They sat in the top row of the newly erected bleachers, ten feet off the ground. Matthew was delighted. If anything could be seen in the fog, it would be seen from there. He sat between Mi and Eloise.

The Prime Minister had been accompanied from Ottawa by his Military Attaché and an Air Vice Marshal. Also by the Deputy Air Minister and the Under-secretary of State for War. Even in spite of the heat, they all wore overcoats.

The Spitfire was due to arrive at 11:00 A.M. It was now 10:50. There had been a lot of band music and a lot of shouting out on the parade ground. Graeme had acquitted himself well during the dreaded inspection of the Guard of Honour. He had walked three paces behind the C.O., dreading an accidental encounter with the P.M.'s heels. Mister King had spoken to three of the men.

Perhaps because of the fog, a great many birds — mostly gulls and pigeons — had decided to spend the morning on the ground. They were everywhere — curious, benign, sedate and oddly quiet. As the party made its way along the ranks, the birds simply stepped aside, as if the Prime Minister's shoes and spats were an everyday encounter.

Graeme had stashed four peppermint candies in his cheeks, so that his one shot of rye would not be noticeable. Or so he prayed.

The Prime Minister was a notorious teetotaller, though Graeme had been relieved to see the Air Vice Marshal accepting a glass of sherry in the mess before they had come out. Just as the inspection was winding to an end and Mister King had concluded his final interview, Graeme bit into one of his candies with too much force and it made a cracking sound like a gun going off. The Prime Minister turned and looked at him and said: "was that you?"

"Yes, sir. I beg your pardon. Just biting into a humbug."

"A peppermint humbug?"

"Yes, sir."

"Have you got another?"

"Yes, sir."

"May I?"

"Please."

Graeme fumbled in his jacket pocket and drew out a small white bag of candies and offered it for the Prime Minister's inspection. There it sat, very white in the palm of Graeme's hand. The C.O. waited patiently and watched all this with amusement.

Every eye in the bleachers — every eye on the reviewing stand — every eye in the nearby ranks followed Mister King's fingers as he reached forward and explored the contents of the bag.

Who could possibly guess what was happening?

They're eating peanuts, was Matthew's conclusion.

Eloise said: "he's going to feed the birds."

Mi laughed out loud. She was so relieved that Graeme hadn't faltered that she wanted to applaud.

Mister King made his selection and popped the humbug into his mouth.

"Ahhh," he said. "Perfectly delicious. I commend you, Forbes."

"Thank you, sir."

Graeme placed the white bag back in his pocket and smoothed the flap. Perspiration rolled into his eyes and he desperately wanted to wipe them. But no such luck. Together with the C.O., he must escort the Prime Minister back to the reviewing stand.

All this while, the band had been playing various stately selections and now it fell silent.

Once the Prime Minister was in place, Graeme saluted him, turned on his heel, faced the ranks and turned the ceremony over to the Parade Commander. It was now 10:58.

All that remained was the arrival of Red Wilson and the Spitfire. Matthew prayed his mother would not ask him to display its toy replica to Eloise. *I lost it,* he would say. Or: *I left it at home.*

Where was Ivan?

At exactly 10:59, the Parade Commander gave the order for all ranks to turn about-face. Other voices echoed this command and Matthew had the dizzying sensation that the whole parade ground was wheeling on a turntable. Even the birds turned a hundred and eighty degrees.

A quiet descended unlike any Matthew had ever experienced. Six or seven hundred people — and not a sound.

The fog looked more and more like drifting smoke. It even had the musty smell of dampened fires.

11:00 A.M.

Where? Where was it?

Off to the right, a low humming vibrato became apparent — a singing, far, far away — then nearer.

All eyes — all heads — turned east.

The vibrato increased. Not a *noise* — not a *sound* — but a thrumming, like a telephone wire in winter, beating against the air.

Mi thought: *bees again. Hornets. Wasps.*

Matthew shivered.

The fog was inscrutable. Blank.

Eloise got out a handkerchief.

The thrumming became a throbbing.

Graeme lifted his head. For the briefest moment, he looked like his old, certain self — alert — erect — alive.

A man in front of Matthew whispered: "quiet."

In the middle ranks, Ivan and Roy stood rows apart, lost in the sea of anonymous backs and white birds.

And then ...

With a *BANG*, it was there.

Slim. Pointed. Its wings atilt and its engine wailing.

Matthew's mouth opened.

Nothing he had ever seen was beautiful, till this.

In the fog and with its camouflage, it had the appearance of a ghost — the spirit, not the body, of an aeroplane.

It streamed — streamed past, so low the shape of Wilson's head was visible inside its glass bubble.

Spit — fire. Spit. Fire.

The plane — it seemed so small — went back inside the fog — its voice scattered — the cleavage of its passage closing after it.

Everyone stopped breathing.

Seconds later, it reappeared, flying higher now — still maintaining the look of an arrow in flight. As it passed the parade ground, Wilson did a victory roll and suddenly everyone in the bleachers cheered.

Hats were thrown in the air. Men and women shouted and waved and sang.

Matthew — spent — sat down.

The wind had a voice. It said: *I am*.

Graeme and Roy had not been able to join them. Wives had not been invited to the mess that night. It was a male event. They were fêting Red Wilson. Matthew was heartbroken, but Mi and Eloise didn't mind so much. They had seen him early in the afternoon, as he was going into lunch with the Prime Minister and his party. Also a male affair — no children, no wives — not even Mary Barker.

"Women don't got no class, I guess," said Eloise.

"They don't want us fawning, that's all."

"I wouldn't fawn," said Eloise. "I'd faint. Lordy, lordy! What a gorgeous man!"

"All heroes are gorgeous. It's part of their stock in trade."

"I'm a sucker for red hair. Always have been."

"Well, you didn't do badly. Roy's pretty gorgeous."

"True. True." Eloise waved her hand. "All he lacks is a Spitfire."

Matthew wished they would talk about something else. Calling men *gorgeous* was embarrassing. It wasn't proper.

They had finished their dinner and Mi and Eloise were drinking coffee and brandy — the brandy supplied by Eloise, who carried a flask. The Green Parrot dining-room was full, but the customers were mostly women — other wives and fiancées who had come for the day's events and been equally banned from the mess.

Eloise said: "I have something to say."

"Say it."

"Uhm ..." Eloise smiled at Matthew. "Are you as bored as you look, chum?"

"Sorry."

"Don't apologize. You have a perfect right to be bored — stuck here with two old women" — Eloise smiled — "when you'd sell your soul to be in that mess with Red Wilson."

"Why don't you go and take a look in the parlour," said Mi. "They usually have some magazines in there. I think they may even have some books."

"Okay." Matthew got down from his place. "I have to go to the bathroom, anyway."

They watched him leave and Mi said: "I hated being that age. Everything bursting inside of you and nothing to be done about it. You're either too young or too old — half child and half something no one has ever been able to define."

"Yes. I remember it well. *What's my body doing to me?*" said Eloise. "And the certainty that everybody knows but you. Do you remember that? *The adult conspiracy?* The feeling that everyone knows something you don't know and they're never going to tell you what it is? As if you're being punished because you're ignorant."

"Yes. And thinking: *I'll kill myself — and then they'll be sorry!*" Mi laughed. "The age of melodrama!"

"How did you plan to do it?"

"I'd throw myself off the roof. Then I'd land on the front walk and be lying there dead when they came home."

"With a rose in your hand!"

"How did you guess!"

"My dear — I always wore my most beautiful dress and spread my ravishing locks as my pillow and lay down, holding a bunch of roses, on the streetcar tracks. The Yonge Street car, of course, and my guilty, dreadful, tormenting parents would be riding on it.

Dead! Dead! Our darling daughter dead! And we *did it!* Oh, it was wonderful. Headlines! Scandal! *Parents Kill Daughter With Streetcar!* Revenge!"

They wound down.

Then Mi said: "I wonder how Matthew plans to kill himself."

Eloise said nothing for a moment. Mi was stirring her coffee — pensive.

"That bad, eh?"

"Yes," said Mi. "Not serious, of course. But he gives the impression he thinks about it. Not being dead — but dying. I feel so sorry for him. He desperately needs a friend. He misses Rupert. Rupert gave him someone to take care of. The way Bonnie did. And he misses Graeme. Even when Graeme is there, he misses him. And ..."

"And?" Eloise sat back and watched. Mi had a story to tell — and wasn't telling it. "And what, Michael?"

"I can't help him, now. At all. Mattie."

"That's nonsense. He adores you."

"Oh, yes. He adores me. But — I'm a dead loss to him. All I think about is ..."

Eloise got out her flask and put more brandy in their cups. Then she said: "all you think about is having an affair?"

Alarmed, Mi said nothing. She lighted a cigarette.

"That's what I'd do, if I was you."

Mi looked away.

"Listen, my darling — your marriage is over. Or might as well be. Don't be embarrassed. I know all about it. Roy says Graeme has behaved like an absolute bastard. Drinking behind everybody's back and screwing that widow. You've been patient. You've been faithful. You've persisted. But now, my dear friend, my advice to you is: *go thou and do likewise*. Find some heavenly young man and get back to living. To being alive. Jesus Christ, Mi — it's what everyone else is doing."

"Is it?"

"You know it is."

"Are you?"

"Don't be ridiculous. I have Roy. We're still in love. Always will be."

"That's what I said. Once."

"Don't get cagey with me, Buster. I know you better than that. You are not a quitter. You still have a life to live. *All* of it."

"Oh ... God."

"Know what someone said to me once, when my father died and the whole damn weight of my dreaded mother fell on me like a ton of bricks, just when I thought I was free at last? This person said to me: *Ellie — when you think you've come to the end of your rope — tie a knot and hang on*."

Mi looked down at her hands on the tablecloth. There was her engagement ring, with its three paste stones.

Eloise laid her hand on top of it.

"You want to know who it was who said that, babe? It was you."

Eloise sat back.

"Take your own advice. Hang on. And if you've forgotten how to tie a knot, come to mama. I'm an expert. Now — having said that — drink your brandy and shut up."

Mi laughed. "Shut up? I haven't said a word."

"Drink your brandy. I have something to tell you."

Mi drank.

Eloise looked at her, beaming. "Ahem," she said. And then: "I'm going to have a baby."

Ivan and Graeme were in their beds. The lights were out. Beyond the windows, the fog was lit with the lamps on the parade ground.

Ivan said: "you have many heroes?"

"One."

"Who was he?"

"My brother. Ian."

Ian.

Ivan.

"The photograph on the bureau?"

"Yes."

Ivan turned on his side. Just the other night he had slept with this man's wife.

"You ever want to be a hero?" he said.

"I was one. Once," said Graeme. His voice sounded oddly sober, for someone who had drunk half a bottle of rye through the evening.

"How do you mean that?"

"Football. Athlete."

"Oh, yeah. The glory days. I remember them."

"You had glory days?"

"Some. I could run. My ambition was to run the marathon. Faster than anyone."

"How close did you come?"

"Nowhere near it. But the ambition felt good. It put me in touch with distance."

"Distance?"

"Yeah. I ran on the prairie. There's a lot of distance there."

"Unh-hunh."

"Then it was motorcycles. Farther and farther — faster and faster."

"Still on the prairie."

"Yep."

"I've never seen it."

"You should. It puts you in your place. Scales you down. Gives you a real sense of size."

"I don't need to be humbled, Ivan."

"No. I know. I didn't mean it that way. I meant — scale. When you understand the scale — how vast distance is — can be — and how small you are — but, being small, how free you are. Take something small with wings and heave it into the sky. A bird is nothing. Nothing, in the scale of things — but the whole sky is open to it. That's what I mean. Taking possession of space — of distance."

"Is that why you fly?"

"I guess." Ivan lay back and watched the ceiling, barely visible — its limits undefined in the pale light. "I want it all," he said. "All of distance, all of space to be mine."

Graeme was silent.

Nothing remained to be said.

In the dark, after Ivan had spoken, Graeme thought: *if only I could run again. If only I could fly. If only I was free of now ... I'd get me to the moon, and never come back. To the moon. Forever. There's distance for you. The only distance that counts. All the way to the moon.*

He slept.

Ivan did not.

In the night, the fog lifted.

In the morning, it was gone. The entire Air Base lay silent, bathed in light.

A wind had risen, cool and scented with sweet grass from the hayfields, recently cut. The land, in that moment just before reveille, was itself again — entirely.

The sole intrusion was the song of a bird. In the sky.

In the night, Matthew had dreamt of flying — not in the Spitfire, but on the motorcycle with Ivan.

The Harley was silent at first, and it slewed from side to side — sliding on a muddy road, unable to gain enough speed for forward movement. Both Matthew and Ivan had to put their feet down at one point and walk it forward, still seated.

Matthew was holding on to Ivan's leather jacket and it was wet and slippery and his fingers kept losing their grip.

Ivan looked back at him and said something that seemed not to be English — something incomprehensible, but said with urgency. Perhaps it was some dream-language version of *hold on tight* or *here we go* or *Heigh-ho, Silver, away!*

The wheels at last gained some purchase in the mud and the Harley began to pick up speed. They were going, it seemed, uphill. Matthew wrapped his arms around Ivan and held on for dear life. When he looked at his arms and down at his thighs, he realized for the first time that he was naked.

The hill grew steeper and the fog began to disperse. Matthew was very conscious of the wind — of the feel of it against his skin and the sound of it in his ears. Ivan pressed back against him and — all at once — the Harley left the ground. It began to climb out into the sky, as if they were emerging from a tunnel — or a cannon.

In school, Matthew had learned of the great horse Pegasus — white and winged — who belonged to the Moon. In the dream, the Harley sprouted wings and carried them, as Pegasus had carried Bellerophon, higher and higher into the sky.

Matthew, in the dream, began to hum — and he could feel the humming's vibrations all through his body as if his innards were singing.

Then, suddenly, the Harley fell.

And did not land.

Matthew woke. He was lying on his stomach — arms and legs spread-eagled as if, in fact, he had been flying.

He pushed himself into a kneeling position.

It had happened again.

He turned and pulled himself to the edge of the bed. He stood up. His groin was cold and wet. He pulled the drawstring and let his pyjama trousers slide to the floor. Then he picked them up and rolled them into a ball.

He went to the bureau and hid them in the bottom drawer underneath his sweater — got out another pair and put them on. Then he went and sat in the window, watching the moon. For the first time in ages — longer than he could remember — he waved, as if the moon were a stranger. *Hello*, he said.

As always, there was no reply.

At nine o'clock, Ivan — in flying gear — crossed the parade ground. He had three students that day and, for once, he dreaded them. Not their clumsiness or their awkwardness, but their necessary presence. He wanted to be alone with the aeroplane. He wanted it to be his.

One of the students, a nineteen-year-old, was called Goodfellow — and lived up to his name. He was born to fly, so it seemed, and his progress through the program had been rapid. There was not an ounce of fear in him — not one intimidated nerve. He would try anything.

But Goodfellows were rare. To some of the students, however eager they were, the complexities of the aeroplanes simply defied them, even now, when they were within eight weeks of achieving their wings. All of these young men were relatively new arrivals from Elementary Flying Training School, where most of their nervousness had been solved through experience. Still, there were some who, whether they hid it or not, were uneasy. Too many dials on the instrument panel — too many subtleties in the weights and measures — too many unpredictables in the aeroplanes's responses to touch. *Less — less. More — more.* The flick of a finger on the wrong knob — the wrong amount of pressure on the rudder pedals — a second's failure of memory during a spin dive — the overzealous use of the throttle — these were all potential killers, and too many students knew it. Not that they didn't try — certainly not that they were cowards — merely that they were baffled. Stymied. That was the hardest part of being an instructor — mustering the patience to break through their bafflement.

On the tarmac, the Harvard Trainer that had been assigned to Ivan stood waiting, its ground crew fussing over a few last details. Goodfellow was there, already geared and 'chuted — a long-toothed grin on his face. The arrival of the Spitfire had obviously had the same effect on him as it had on Ivan.

"Morning."

"Morning."

"Beaut of a day for it."

"Yeah."

They had to yell all this, because some of the other trainers were already moving out onto the runway and their engines had a particularly raucous sound to them.

Once he had been helped into his parachute, Ivan turned to Goodfellow and yelled: "I'm going up alone."

"What?"

"I'M GOING UP ALONE."

"WHY? IN THE FLIGHT OFFICE YOU SAID IT WAS MY TURN."

"SURE. BUT THERE'S SOMETHING I WANT TO SHOW YOU, FIRST."

"THEN I'LL COME WITH YOU."

"NO. I WANT YOU TO SEE IT FROM THE GROUND."

Goodfellow nodded. He was obviously disappointed, but he accepted the situation and stepped back.

Ivan gave him the high sign and Goodfellow returned it.

Five minutes later, Ivan was in the air — six thousand feet above the runways.

He was going to break every rule in the book. He was going to push himself all the way to the edge and show them once and for all that he was ready for Ops — that his too many days and weeks and months of instructing others were over — that he was wasted on Harvards and ready for Spitfires.

Yes — it would get him into trouble — but one way out of trouble was to force them to send you overseas, where dancing with danger was welcome. You had to prove that nothing could intimidate you — and you had to do it with grace and control and discipline. And with flair. Besides, he was too good a pilot to waste and he knew they knew that. That was what he had told himself, even though part of him knew it was wrong. *But to hell with it being wrong*, he had said to himself in the mirror that morning. *I want — I want to do this, and I'm going to do it.*

At eight thousand feet, he levelled off.

Somewhere below him, Mi might be watching. Certainly his ground crew was watching. And Goodfellow. Word would have spread that he was up there alone on what should have been an instruction flight. *Henderson. Solo.*

There was the sky. It was his.

The joy of it. The mad expanse. The longest, widest playing field in Creation.

Mine.

He looked down.

He counted over what he meant to do.

Spin, first.

Level off.

Fly-past.

Victory roll.

Red Wilson be damned.

Ivan recited the instructions he had given others a hundred times or more: *you will now do a spin to the right — and the recovery.*

He throttled back — pulling up the nose of the Harvard — *but not all the way to stalling speed.*

Full rudder to the right.

Power off.

And away we go.

Free fall.

He dropped four thousand feet.

Spinning.

Yelling his head off.

This was glory — and all he knew of it.

Something shook loose.

His mind went blank.

Mi said: "what was that?"

Nella said: "there's smoke."

Agnes said: "it's black."

Matthew said: *it's Ivan.*

But not out loud.

Roy came to tell them. He stood in the yard with his hat in his hand and apologized. What he had to say was hurtful and difficult.

Had Graeme been in the plane, as he was before? How many deaths? One or two? And whose?

Mi stopped listening after Roy's first sentence. Of course she knew what he was saying — it had all been said in her mind, while they waited for the phone to ring. When it hadn't rung, she had begun to think she might be wrong — but she did not believe it. Ivan himself would have phoned just to say: *it wasn't me.* But it was.

Her mind was drowning, incoherent — afraid of concentration. It splashed around in a lake of song lyrics, movie dialogue and midnight conversations. Images of Ivan floated to the surface, turned their back on her and sank.

There had been no tears. Not one. Matthew had kicked the wall and run away; angry.

Mi was angry, too — or part of her was. One voice said: *you bastard! How dare you do this!* — and another voice said: *don't.* She had played all her records — every one — trying to make the voices stop.

Poor Roy. He didn't know what he was saying. However sorry he was, he had no idea that he was saying anything more than: *your friend is dead. Your husband's room-mate.*

Graeme's room-mate.

That's right. He was Graeme's room-mate. I'd forgotten ...

"You bastard."

That, she had spoken aloud.

How?

Roy had said: *I didn't see it.*

How? Tell me how.

The wings fell off. Pulling out of a dive.

Fell off?

Stress. Some undetected damage from a previous flight. Could be. Who knows?

Was he with a student?

No. He was alone.

I see.

Graeme wasn't mentioned. Why mention Graeme? Graeme was alive.

Is. And so am I. Damn it.

Mi had kissed Roy and thanked him for coming. There was a driver in the staff car. Mi nodded at him and went back into the house to find Matthew.

Now, it was evening.

Something must be said. To Graeme. She owed him that. Condolences. And Matthew must go with her. Solidarity. Us. We three.

Everybody loved him. *The whole bloody fucking world* had been in love with Ivan.

Don't.

Mi phoned Eloise. Eloise would come and take them.

Matthew was on the porch with Hunter and Nella. Nella had the wisdom not to speak. In her own times of sorrow, she had wanted silence. Words were crude. Intrusive. *Sorry means nothing.*

When Mi shut the screen door, Nella looked up and nodded.

Mi said: "Matthew?"

Matthew did not reply.

"Matthew?"

"Yes, ma'am."

"We're going to go and see Dad."

"No."

"Yes. I know how you feel ..."

"No, you don't."

"I know how you feel and we must. We owe it to Ivan."

"Why?"

"Because Dad was his room-mate. There wasn't anyone else. Isn't. He doesn't have a single relative."

Matthew stood up.

"What should I wear?"

"You can go like that. We're just going to stay half an hour. Eloise is coming to take us."

"Okay. I'll go and pee."

Leaving, he banged the door. Miss Rose had taught him well.

Mi went to the top step.

Nella watched her.

She's a brave, decent woman. To look at her, you wouldn't know a thing.

"Nella?"

"Yes?"

Mi's back was to her — rigid.

"Thank you."

Then she turned and there were tears.

Nella said nothing. She cocked her head and, watching Mi, she nodded three times. *Don't even mention it, my dear. Don't say a word. I understand.*

Mi got out her handkerchief and went down the steps. When Eloise arrived, Mi's eyes were dry.

At the gate, the guard let them drive on through. Mi had looked the other way as they passed the field where Ivan's plane had crashed. Matthew saw it, inadvertently. A salvage crew and some trucks surrounded what remained of the fuselage. It was still smoking. There was a fire truck.

At the Admin Building, Eloise let them out and said: "I'll wait for you here."

Up the steps and through the doors.

It would never be the same.

Down the corridor.

"See if he's in his room."

The door was closed.

Matthew knocked.

Mi did not want to go in. She was afraid of seeing Ivan's things — his possessions. Whatever they were. A silver-backed brush. A photograph.

What else?

"He's not there."

"All right. He'll be in the mess."

All the way to the end.

The ante-room. The hats.

In the mess, the atmosphere was subdued.

Mi had been certain Graeme would be drunk. But he wasn't. He was standing alone on the terrace. Sober.

Sue Anne?

Thank God, no.

Some of the officers turned as Mi and Matthew passed. No one spoke. Perhaps there was a protocol.

The barman nodded gravely.

The air was warmer outside than in. There was a hint of smokiness. A residue.

The Bay had sailboats on it. Two of them.

When Bonnie died, there had been a sailboat. One. Now two.

"Graeme."

He turned.

Mi thought: *oh, dear God.*

He was desolate. Old. Dead.

She walked all the way up to him and put her arms around him and kissed him on the cheek. His body had no resistance to it. It was merely there.

Very slowly, he raised his arms from his sides and completed the embrace.

Matthew watched.

Mi and Graeme separated.

Graeme said: "thank you for coming."

Mi said nothing. She patted his arm.

Graeme smiled at Matthew.

"Hi, chief."

"Hi."

Graeme beckoned to Matthew and put his hand on his shoulder.

"Good for you," he said. "This is hard."

"Yessir."

Then Graeme let go and, for a moment, they all stood watching the sailboats.

"They'll be coming in soon."

"Someone you know?"

"Yes. One of them is the C.O. The other is a sailing partner of Ivan's."

There. Said.

"Whenever there's been an accident" — *a death* — "the C.O. goes out there to ease the tension. Not a bad idea."

A very good idea. I wish we were there.

After a moment, Graeme rested his arms against the railing and said: "look — let's not talk about it now. Let's just ... remember him."

Mi nodded.

Graeme turned then and looked at Matthew. He put his hand in his pocket and drew something out. "You must have forgotten this the other night," he said — and closed his hand over Matthew's. "Your Spitfire. I found it on Ivan's bureau."

Matthew stared.

It was not his. His Spitfire was broken. Scattered below them.

Matthew looked at Mi.

Her back was to him.

Mum?

Graeme said: "the funeral is on Friday."

That was the end of it. They all went inside and Graeme walked them to Eloise and the car.

15th August, 1942

They did not go in. They stood outside the fence and watched from there.

Matthew wore his blazer. Mi wore blue. It seemed proper.

The parade ground already had people on it. Not as many as had come to see the Spitfire, but more than a hundred. On the other side of the road, and everywhere else on the base, business went on as usual. It had to. The war.

There were three flights of men and one of women. They stood at ease, facing west, where the reviewing stand had been set.

All the flags were at half-mast.

There were no birds. Not one.

The Parade Commander gave an order — and everyone snapped to attention.

Band music was heard. The "Dead March" from *Saul*. Mi told Matthew what it was called. He had never heard anything so solemn before.

Graeme, stepping in slow time, entered from somewhere beyond the barracks where Matthew had seen the man with the falling cigarette. Behind him, the escort party — also stepping in time — followed in marching order. Thirty-five, Matthew counted — all with black armbands.

As they made their way onto the parade ground, others came after. The band, the bearer party, the supporting party and the firing party. Aircraftsmen, carrying rifles with bayonets fixed — two men with bugles, led by a Sergeant ...

The band, all playing — and the drummers drumming ...

Six young Officers ... three on one side, three on the other, step-step-stepping, as the flat-bed truck bearing Ivan's coffin was driven to its place before the reviewing stand.

Matthew's hand went up as if to wave. *There he is.*

The Air Force Ensign, with Ivan's cap on top of it, was draped across the casket.

Matthew pushed his fingers through the links of the fence.

Mi said nothing. She was standing at attention.

The C.O. marched alone with the Chaplain, peeling off and moving to the reviewing stand, where he faced the parade ground.

Graeme gave an indecipherable command. All they could hear was the distant, unmistakable sound of his voice.

Everyone saluted.

Graeme shouted.

Everyone stood at ease.

Everyone but Mi.

The Chaplain stepped forward. Some sort of prayer was said.

An aeroplane flew overhead.

There was a pause.

Graeme shouted something else.

The firing party stood forward.

The band began to play. A hymn.

Now, the Sergeant of the firing party shouted.

The airmen raised their rifles at the sky.

Abide with me, fast falls the eventide.

VOLLEY!

The darkness deepens; Lord, with me abide.

VOLLEY!

When other helpers fail, and comforts flee,

VOLLEY!

Help of the helpless, O abide with me!

The hymn continued. And concluded.

Matthew moved along the fence, his fingers leading. The links made pictures, framed in diamonds — snapshots, askew, of what he saw.

Ivan.

Don't.

His fingers hurt.

They were bleeding.

The firing party buglers played "The Last Post" in tandem.

Matthew froze.

There was a silence.

Everyone was locked in position.

Ten seconds passed.

The wind blew.

The buglers played reveille.

When it was done, Mi went and stood behind Matthew. She put her hands on his shoulders, lightly. *I am here. All is well.*

The bearer party stepped forward.

Ivan's cap and the Ensign were removed from his coffin, and the Ensign — with great formality — was folded until it was so small it could barely be seen.

When this was done, the truck moved slowly forward, making for the gates. Ivan's body, kindness of his grandfather, was to be returned to Saskatchewan — to the prairie — to the sky.

Mi watched it go and turned towards Graeme.

He was rigid. No more the boy — only the man. His body, at last, had achieved the dignity too long denied it. Mi thought: *he's come back, but it's too late.*

The band played "Men of Harlech." A quick-march. No more dying, only living. Only being alive. The funeral was over.

16th August, 1942

Mi woke at seven-thirty, perhaps to the sound of Alvin and Alex driving away in their truck. Lying there in her bed, she thought: *it's a new world, today. Depopulated by one.*

Eloise was going to have a baby.

Good.

She had barely slept. Most of the night, she had sat in the window and watched her bed in the moonlight. It was empty. There was no one there — its coverlet, folded down — its pillows, piled against the headboard, sagging. They had looked like two elderly women sound asleep, sitting up. The top sheet had been drawn back — waiting. Mi had thought: *beds are catafalques. The dead lie there with the living and the living dream of the dead.*

Then she had crossed the room and lain there. Alone.

Now, it was morning.

The sun was shining. *Cruel*, she thought. *It shouldn't be allowed.*

She stood up.

I'm going to have a drink.

    I beg your pardon?

    I'm going to have a drink.

    It's seven-thirty in the morning!

    Fuck off.

The bottle was in the bureau — middle drawer.

She took the glass from her carafe and filled it half full with rye.

There, in the centre of the bureau top — surrounded by hair brushes, combs and perfume bottles — was the Spitfire. Ivan's.

Matthew.

Mi heard herself speak. Not a word, but something like a word, caught halfway through her lips and swallowed.

She put her hand up flat against her mouth.

Then she reached out and touched the Spitfire.

He knows. Knew. Knows.

Yes.

Mi lifted the glass and drank.

In the barnyard, Hunter barked.

Downstairs, the front door opened and Miss Rose departed for the Crazy Wing.

The Crazy Wing.

Wings.

His wings fell off.

Down. Because of some undetected damage. Stress. In that case, all our wings are going to fall.

Mi drank.

There was the Spitfire.

Zoom!

He'd said that. *Zoom!*

Mi went back to the bed. She put the glass on the table, stubbed her cigarette and climbed in under the sheet.

The Spitfire was in her hand.

She lay with it against the pillows.

That evening, Mi took Nella and Matthew to dinner at The Green Parrot, with Eloise.

Nella wore a green velvet gown and a ribbon around her neck. With her straight-cut hair, the ribbon and puffed sleeves, she looked like a child.

She handed an envelope to Matthew.

"Open it later," she said. "And here's something for you." Nella handed Mi a package. Wrapped in plain brown paper, it had *Michael* written on it with a thick-nibbed pen.

"Am I to wait, too?"

"Yes. I just thought, the occasion called for gift-giving."

"Thank you."

"I'm sorry I don't have anything for Mrs Best."

"Not to worry." Eloise smiled.

Nella said: "Michael always keeps her promises. She said some weeks ago she would take me to dinner here — and here we are."

"Yes."

Sue Anne was sitting across the room with another woman. She looked herself again, spritely and — a word Mi hated — *pert.*

Good for her. Up and at 'em! World without end.

Sue Anne did not see her. Or gave that impression.

Matthew said: "I had a letter from Rupert today."

"Did you?" said Mi. "I didn't know that."

"You were asleep."

"What did it say?"

"It said: *I'm in Argentina.*"

"Good heavens! He certainly gets around. Will he be going back to school?"

"Yes."

"That's good. You'll certainly have a lot to talk about."

"Yes."

Matthew subsided. Then he said: "yes," again.

Mi looked at him and smiled.

I'm alive. I have a son to prove it.

That night, she opened her package and found Nella's scarf —

245

and a note. The note said: *this is for you to keep. In memory.*

My flag.

Mi went down to Matthew's room.

"Good night," she said.

"Good night."

Nella's gift to Matthew was sitting on his bureau. It was a water-colour — all in blue — with two white birds in the sky.

Underneath, Nella had written: *HEROES.*

That was all.

One more photograph in the box. It shows a farmhouse porch, with what appears to be a family gathered for their portrait. An older woman in an apron, her husband in his overalls, both standing in front of the door — the grandparents, stern and loving. Two eccentric aunts — one in a wide-brimmed hat and smock, the other in a nurse's uniform. They sit in rocking chairs. A young woman, standing, leans against the railing. She is smiling. Happy. A boy is seated halfway down the steps, a stick in his hand — a dog beside him. The daughter, who had left home early for the city, now returning to show off her son.

Two hard-working men, booted, are seated on the top step, their Thermos bottles beside them, their lunch pails cradled in their laps. It is late afternoon; the sun shines brightly on their faces. The uncle — the brother, looking sad.

Chickens scratch in the dust of the walk. The dog is panting, eyes half-closed. The clapboard walls of the house, the roof above — a testament. Here is peace in the midst of conflict — plenty in the midst of loss. Here is home and home is everything.

Leaning out towards them, slim and attenuated, is the shadow of the man who takes the photograph. He is uniformed and wears his cap. A motorcycle tips its spoked front wheel and its handlebars into the lower right-hand corner of the picture. Its surfaces gleam. Its name is Pegasus.

The sun, descending, levels its rays on the boy's face. His eyes are shining, his mouth shut tight. He seems to be holding his breath and watching something no one else can see. Words come to mind — tomorrow — later — someday.

This is all there is. The final fragment, delicate with age. One perfect moment. Caught forever — and left behind.